RANDOM ACTS OF BLINDNESS

One life. So many stories.

David Random

Printed in the United States of America

ISBN: Softcover   978-1-63871-356-2
        eBook   978-1-63871-357-9

Republished by: PageTurner Press and Media LLC
Publication Date: 07/21/2021

To order copies of this book, contact:

PageTurner Press and Media
Phone: 1-888-447-9651
info@pageturner.us
www.pageturner.us

To Fran,
my classmate and
friend. Enjoy the
stories. I look
forward to seeing you
soon at Kimball's.

Love,

David
2024

The Stories

Random Acts of Blindness

Having been born with the last name Random, every-thing I do has, at one time or another, been jokingly referred to as such. Although these references were meant as a play on words by high school classmates and other friends, the unplanned, haphazard and "random" nature with which I perform many activities would seem to suggest that the dictionary definition of the word might also prove to be unavoidably true.

The "random acts of blindness" to which I refer attests to a long list of observable phenomena which I have trouble seeing. I don't mean to suggest that my eyes are incapable of vision. I see things just fine. It's simply the *logic* of certain things I sometimes fail to see. In the scheme of things these are not with any degree of consequence. Whether I see these things or not matters little. My blindness has no effect beyond my puzzled mind. No one's life hangs in the balance. The earth will not disintegrate because of my failure to perceive the logic of something that seems to defy common sense. Nevertheless, there remains a host of things I just don't see.

I don't see why a pizza establishment is called a "pizzeria" instead of a "pizzaria." They don't sell pizzers.

They sell pizzas. I also don't see why the word "gubernatorial" is used rather than the more logical "governatorial." There are only a handful of states in which their lame-brained governor would be more appropriately labeled a "guber."

Then there's the side dish made from shredded cabbage and mayonnaise, not cooked, but served chilled. I don't see why it's called coleslaw and not more appropriately labeled "coldslaw." Even as a kid, I thought that just made more sense. Until I learned how to spell, I actually thought it *was* called coldslaw.

I also don't see why dead people are called "late." These people are never going to be on time for anything ever again. Punctuality will not be their strong suit. Get over it.

I don't see why the legal copy at the end of nearly every pharmaceutical ad on TV must include the warning "*do not take this medicine if you are allergic to this medicine.*" If they think we're that dumb, maybe they'd make more money selling "stupid pills."

And I don't see why when you do something again, but with more conviction, you're said to "redouble" your efforts. Don't you have to double your effort before you can redouble it? What am I not seeing here?

Yes, there are a lot of things I just don't see. When I was a kid, every TV episode of Superman, for example, began with a crowd of bystanders gathered on a city sidewalk craning their necks to look skyward. Various people would shout with great excitement about something flying high above them. "Look! Up in the sky," one would shout. Looking up, another would loudly proclaim, "It's a BIRD!" Still others would yell "It's a PLANE!!! It's SUPERMAN!!!"

Okay, I'll admit, if I saw a man in a cape flying high above the city I'd get excited too. But here's where my blindness kicks in. I don't see why the first two people who thought it was a bird or a plane got so excited. I just don't see it.

And I fail to see why my grades in high school were either A, B, C, D, or... F. What happened to E? I would gladly have traded my D in algebra for an E in order to convince my parents that it stood for "Excellent."

Nor do I see why the government still makes pennies despite the fact that, according to the U.S. mint, each penny costs over two cents to make. The collection of pennies free for the taking at the checkout counter of every supermarket would seem to suggest that these little disks have no value, and are little more than an inconvenience. If I were president, I'd stop the production of these outdated relics and use the money saved to pay off the national debt. (After rounding it off to the nearest nickel of course.)

And speaking of things that are free, I fail to see the logic of a recent on-line offer promising me a "free gift" if I signed up and paid for a new software package. Last I knew, all gifts were free. Isn't that what a gift is? Yet I'll only receive this free gift if I give them money. Am I the only one who doesn't see this?

Nor do I see why someone is said to sleep like a baby when babies wake up and cry three times a night. Or why we say someone is as happy as a clam. I've studied clams in close proximity. They don't look all that cheerful.

And I don't see why doctors are said to "practice" medicine. I don't mind having my lawn mowed by someone who is not yet at the top of their game. But I would hope that someone cutting into me with a scalpel has already had enough practice to be handed a sharp instrument after correctly identifying the location of the spleen.

Nor do I see why we never hear about "second-world" countries. We hear about third-world countries all the time. But I fail to see why we seem to have skipped over those that, I presume, are only slightly less advanced than our own. Is it because we don't want to destroy the illusion that there could possibly be some who are almost as good as we are? I'm sorry, but I just don't see it.

I don't see how skunks can stand their own smell. I don't see why you can't tickle yourself, or why men have nipples. And I don't see why there's a permanent press setting on my iron.

And I don't see why the first person to ever buy a telephone decided to make such a useless purchase. Who did he think he was going to call anyway?

I also don't see why there are Interstate highways in Hawaii, why the Easter Bunny carries chicken eggs, why we drive on parkways but park on driveways, or why, on Labor Day, we honor work by not working.

I could go on and on about all the things I just don't see. But I just don't see what good that would do.

Childhood Challenges

Of all the challenges I overcame as a kid, the most formidable had to be lima beans. "Just two more bites," Mom would insist. She might as well have said "two more plates full."

I tried hiding them in my mashed potatoes, hoping I would be excused for not finishing what everyone knew was there more for decoration anyway.

I chewed them until they were dry and could not swallow. I chewed and chewed until I thought I would gag. In a stroke of genius one evening, I asked to be excused to go to the bathroom where I promptly spit them out. I waited for what I thought was an appropriate length of time, then flushed. Proud of my resourcefulness, I returned to the table and to my father's sideways grin that seemed to say, "I used to pull that trick when I was a kid, too."

Mealtime was always full of challenges. For some reason, I seemed to be the only person at the table who found bones in my fish. By the end of the meal, the lineup of tiny, white splinters on the side of my plate made it look like I was building a picket fence. Was I the only one who was chewing his food? Was the rest of the family just gulping down huge unchewed mouthfuls without a thorough exploration of what had just been transported on the end of his fork? I became so obsessed with each bite that, I swear, by the second grade, I was sure I could find bones in Jell-O.

As challenging as mealtime was, however, bedtime was a close second. As a very young child, when my family moved into an old house in the suburbs west of Boston, I was relegated to a bedroom on the ground floor while the rest of the family slept comfortably upstairs. What I heard during the night as I lay awake, alone with an entire floor to myself, made lima beans seem like child's play. In the dead of night, the two-hundred-year-old structure took on a life of its own. The creaks and groans of ancient floor boards settling under their own weight became the footsteps of imagined creatures. Bottles inside the refrigerator rattled by the vibration of the motor became chains being dragged across the floor toward my isolated corner of the house. No matter how many times I yelled for my father to run downstairs and turn on the light, having arrived, he could not convince me otherwise. I suspect it was my frequent, middle-of-the-night calls for help that eventually allowed me to graduate to an upstairs room that I shared with my baby sister. The creaks and groans of our aging house still persisted, but I rationalized that any monster looking for a small child to snack on would surely select my younger, and therefore, more tender sibling.

As I got older, challenges became less imagined and more consequential. Because I was always very artistic and liked to draw pictures, that side of my brain became more developed. As a result, the opposite side of my brain, starved for stimulation and exercise, began to diminish. It was a new form of endeavor called mathematics that challenged this neglected part of my brain and became my downfall. I had little trouble with simple addition and subtraction. As long as I could count my fingers I was fine. When numbers got so high that I ran out of fingers to count, I simply started counting other more numerous things. Crayons, pieces of candy, lima beans.

Then came fourth grade. And with it, long division. No longer able to rely on finger-counting to determine the answer to thirty-six divided by eight, I was completely baffled. With no personal calculators in those days, I was compelled to utilize the under-developed, analytical side of my brain to decipher such complicated mathematical problems that now lay before me. I muddled my way through grade-school arithmetic only to discover a higher form of torture called algebra waiting to ambush me in high school.

All things considered, I realize how lucky I've been and how my childhood challenges pale by comparison to what others experience. I grew up in a loving home and, while we were far from rich, we certainly were not poor. We took vacations and we always had enough to eat. We were certainly more fortunate than many other people in the world. I remember my mother telling me that there were poor children starving in Africa.

"Okay," I'd tell her. "I'll send them my lima beans."

You Are What You Wear

"I'm never going to be a ghost again."

I was six years old when I made this emphatic declaration. It was Halloween night and we had just returned home from what should have been a delightfully spooky candy-gathering expedition. Despite having collected a pillowcase full of treats, it was clear to my mother that I was not happy.

"What's wrong?" she asked.

Using my best skills at over-acting, I demonstrated to her how the sheet that covered my small frame shifted with every movement. The simple act of turning my head caused the eye-holes to shift to the side. It took only a small gust of wind to push the sheet up around my waist revealing my sneakers and pants, allowing people to realize that I was actually just a little kid wearing a sheet. I felt I was not fooling anyone. Not to mention the fact that my attempt to eat a fudge-sicle through the narrow mouth slit did not go well at all. After throwing my stash of candy onto the kitchen floor in a melodramatic display of temper, I yanked the sheet off and in so doing, became entangled in the fudge-stained garment.

"Tommy was a pirate," I complained. "Next year I want

to be a pirate. I'll bet Tommy could see where he was going even with his eye patch. And pirates can eat fudgesicles!"

Although, as years went by, I remember no subsequent attempt to persuade people that I was, in fact, a lawless plunderer of the high seas, this would not be the last time I used wardrobe to define myself. Throughout the years, in fact, it happened quite frequently. Even if I was the only person who was ultimately convinced of the authenticity of my cowboy hat and toy pistol, it was worth the hours of nagging it took to persuade my parents of the necessity of such attire.

And that plastic fireman's hat my grandmother gave me for my birthday probably did little to fool my friends into believing that I had somehow obtained employment in the local fire department as a seven-year-old.

Nevertheless, over the years, wardrobe would continue to be a key ingredient in portraying myself as the alter-ego to which I aspired. When I was in high school, I formed a rock band with several other students who, as I did, envisioned themselves as local celebrities causing girls to swoon and boys to be in awe. The Torqués, as we were known, featured an impressive array of electric instruments, drums, and amplifiers. Our music was a big hit at school dances in the 1960s. But it was our matching outfits that caused people to believe we might have been more than just a local phenomenon. It was our tailored light blue suits and stylish, pencil-thin ties that helped convince people that we actually *were* the image we tried to project. As far as they knew, maybe our reputation extended far beyond their limited awareness, and perhaps we were as popular in more distant areas as well, but the fact that they had not yet seen us on TV was because they had simply tuned in to the wrong channels.

I always considered myself lucky that the dress code in my school was not particularly strict. Of course there were certain regulations to which we were required to adhere. I can still hear the principal, Mr. Grey, yell out, *"Tuck in that shirt, young man!"* In the scheme of things, however, the attitude was pretty tolerant. There were no school uniforms and few mandatory wardrobe considerations. Shirts had to be buttoned within one button of the top. And students could not wear blue jeans. Other than that, pretty much anything was allowed. To be fair, girls had more wardrobe restrictions placed on them than boys. But for the most part, common sense prevailed. There was one instance when I was reprimanded for wearing sandals on a particularly hot day, despite there being no specific rule banning them. While I subsequently complied with this unwritten rule, I felt compelled to create a sign which I prominently displayed on the table in front of me during sixth-period study hall. It featured a large drawing of a pair of sandals with the caption, "If they're good enough for Jesus, they're good enough for me." While I was still not allowed to wear sandals, my sign was never challenged.

The clothing we wear goes a long way in helping to create our image. It can make you look successful, fun, athletic, even weird if that's the look you're after. Ever since I was old enough to select my own clothes, my wardrobe helped me become who I pretended to be.

It was not always, however, to convince others of a pseudo-identity. Sometimes the clothes we wore were just an attempt to be in style and to fit in. When I was in junior high school, penny loafers were all the rage. One was considered out of touch if he didn't keep up with the trend by wearing shoes that featured a leather slot into which you could wedge a shiny, copper coin.

In the 1970s, no one in his right mind would have chosen to wear what fashion designers persuaded us was fashionable. But that's exactly what we did. Looking back at photos from that era makes me wonder why anyone thought bell-bottom pants were a good idea. But the one saving grace of bell-bottoms was that it didn't matter what shoes you wore with them. You could even wear the now-out-of-style penny loafers and no one would know. No one could see them under that flowing umbrella of material that made it look as if you were sweeping a path in front of yourself as you walked.

Pants weren't the only thing that got wider in the seventies. The skinny neckties I wore in my rock group only a decade earlier were now suddenly passé. Ties became continually wider forcing us to constantly modify our accessories wardrobe just to remain in style. Psychedelic colors and designs were also making their initial appearance on neckties which, by the mid-seventies, were so wide they began to resemble kites. Like bell-bottoms, however, there was also a benefit to the new trend in neckwear in that it drew attention away from the hair styles of the seventies. Looking at photos from that era, it's the hair that most screams out, *"I know I look ridiculous, but someday we'll all have a good laugh about this."*

The best thing about the seventies was that they ended. It had taken us an entire decade to realize that there were, in fact, no redeeming qualities about much of what we called fashion.

Upon graduating from college and joining the workforce, I found myself confined to a narrowing spectrum of acceptable styles. Although I was in an industry where creativity was encouraged, there were still those days on which I would be required to meet with suit-wearing clients who took their jobs seriously. I found that, on my limited budget, I needed two distinct wardrobes—one to appear serious in front of clients, and another to be accepted by my peers. Co-workers could always tell when I had a client meeting. It looked as though I was dressing for a funeral.

Over the decades, dress codes relaxed. Casual Fridays became casual everydays. There were still a few client-meeting days on which I chose, of my own accord, to wear a sports coat. The tie, however, was usually left at home and reserved for occasions on which there actually *was* a funeral.

Years have passed and I find myself no longer bound by the whims of fashion. I am at that point in my life where I wear what I want when I want to wear it. I am not trying to be anything that I'm not. There are, of course, occasions for which I will shed my jeans for dressier pants and lose the slightly worn shirt for one that looks less than ten years old. This is usually preceded by my wife casually asking, "Is *that* what you're going to wear?"

I sometimes wonder if there will come a time when today's young adults will look back at their long-forgotten photographs and question the reasoning behind their fashion choices that included pre-ripped jeans and backward baseball caps. It's not that I'm judging, but back when I was still wearing bell-bottoms, I knew enough that when they started to rip in more than three places, it was time for them to go. If I'm still around when the next generation blindly follows the questionable trends of the day, don't be surprised if you hear me ask some fad-conscious teen on his way to a party, "Is *that* what you're going to wear?"

Count Me Out

W ell, I've made it through another year without once having to use algebra. The countless hours I sat listening to Mister Cummings attempt to explain the coefficients of variable exponents proved to be a complete waste of time. I always suspected as much. When I questioned my seventh-grade math teacher about when the need for such a convoluted and un-intelligible discipline might be necessary, he just grinned. In eighth grade I posed the same question to the same teacher. As unaccustomed as math teachers are to using verbal skills, this time he was able to respond using words.

"Trust me," he said, "you'll find these disciplines will come in handy later in life."

This time, it was me who found no words to respond. I simply stared at him with a skeptical look on my face.

Mister Cummings continued. "How will you ever be-come a math teacher if you don't know these fundamentals?"

This time, I remember laughing out loud. The prospect of my becoming a math teacher was about as far-fetched as my pitching for the Boston Red Sox. And if your only need for learning algebra is to be able to teach these mental gymnastics to other confused kids, I seriously question its value. If I could have dropped out of the class I would have done so in a heartbeat. But given that junior high school math is not an elective course, I was resigned to taking up otherwise valuable space in the classroom for the remainder of the year. Who cares if "X" divided by "Y" equals three hundred and forty eight. It was hard enough performing these types of problems with numbers, but now they've been turned into riddles. Now there are letters where the numbers should be and I have to guess what the numbers are. I might have had an easier time understanding hieroglyphics.

Although counting (or any other kind of math) has never been my strong point, I can count on the fingers of one hand the times I've had to use anything remotely resembling algebra. Actually, it's math in general that has always been my downfall. I'm okay at simple addition and subtraction. I get plenty of practice balancing my checkbook. Mostly subtraction. And now that every phone has a built-in calculator, I no longer need to take up valuable brain space to figure out that 1,427 minus 989 equals 4... wait a minute. Let me turn my calculator on.

Luckily, in the fifty-plus years since graduation, my life has been one in which the need for math has been minimal. All through my career, my focus has been on the visual arts. If a client had to be billed for my hours of service, there were other people whose job it was to figure that out. It's another part of the brain entirely that sees numbers as a meaningful vocabulary, and I am in awe of those that are able to do so.

Perhaps the most frustrating and head-spinning annual math ritual is that of tax preparation. The stacks of papers covered with confusing numbers spread out on the table in front of me are the most confounding thing I can imagine. If my life depended on it, I'd sooner take my chances deciphering an electroencephalogram of my own brain prior to brain surgery rather than trying to make sense of itemized transactional deductions of renumerated revenue depreciation. Peering into the scans of my own brain couldn't be any more complicated than doing taxes. At least I wouldn't see any numbers in there.

I don't mean to say that I excelled at every other subject in school. After four years of French I knew only enough of the language to finally be able to ask what time it was. I was not approaching anything resembling fluency. Under my senior photo in the high school yearbook is the caption, "*Dave, Parlez vous Francais?*" Someday I'll look that up and see what it means.

There were a few kids who graduated from high school with me who excelled at math. I've always wondered what those kids who went on to major in mathematics did with the rest of their lives. I mean, given that we already have enough math teachers to last a while, I picture them now sitting at office desks piled high with papers, sleeves rolled up and incessantly punching the keys of calculators trying to determine the value of "X" and "Y." I imagine them constantly utilizing algebra to figure out every aspect of their very precise lives. How much water to add to the rice if you're making three and one-eighth servings. How to mow their lawns with the fewest number of passes. Or how much time to allow to drive to the grocery store if you're driving at forty-eight miles per hour for the first seven miles, and thirty-four miles per hour for the remaining six and a half miles.

I am grateful for the fact that I've lived a life in which

I have not had to figure out math riddles using letters instead of numbers. My enjoyment of life has not been diminished because I was one of those people who just didn't get the math gene.

I guess it's true when they say there are only three kinds of people in the world. Those that are good at math, and those that aren't.

My Life in Shades of Gray

I grew up in black and white. My childhood photos will confirm this. Page after page of the family album depicts my early life in glorious shades of gray. There I am in my striped jersey, light gray and dark gray, on my gray and white tricycle in front of our dark gray house. And that's me standing in our gray backyard among tall, gray grass in front of beautiful gray flowers.

Several pages of the album attest to the fact that, in those early years, even our Christmas trees were gray. Shiny, gray ornaments sparkle from garland-laden, gray boughs under which a veritable landscape of Christmas presents are displayed in the most festive, gray gift-wrap.

The pages of my family album will also tell you that I descended from a long line of gray people. Parents, grandparents, and great-grandparents all frozen in time, totally unconcerned that their preservation would necessitate the draining of color from their rosy cheeks, colorful picnics, and family gatherings.

The interesting thing is that those memories are not diminished by their lack of color. Quite the opposite, in fact, seems to be the case. Over time, it is the memories of my black and white days that I find are the most colorful. Those sweet moments and happy celebrations faithfully preserved in the photos of my youth form a rich tapestry of memories that become more vivid even as the photographs fade. Perhaps it is because the very grayness itself forces me to use my imagination all the more, while the cheap color snapshots that came decades later rob me of the need to remember. In those gaudy drugstore prints of subsequent years, every detail is vividly preserved in glossy Kodacolor, so there's no need to remember the color of our family car. Or what shade of blue my favorite shirt was. Because my mind doesn't have to fill in the missing pieces of the picture, my memory is not as actively engaged. Yet in those very early prints from decades before my existence, I find myself trying to imagine the colors of my great grandmother's shawl and the rich spectrum of her backyard garden.

The fact that the early images exist only as colorless reproductions also reinforces the fact that they represent moments from an earlier era. Their lack of color is a reminder that they are substantially removed from the reality of the present moment, receding into a distant past marked not only by lack of color, but by an extended period of time. It is as if the passing of time itself, like a fading memory, is responsible for the loss of color. And only through memory can it be restored. The desire to recall more vividly those distant events, those aged picnics, long-ago houses, and former friends is what brings the pages of my family albums remarkably to life.

The grayness seems not out of place when recalling my childhood. It was a monochromatic world back then, and to a certain extent, the early photos accurately captured real life. The dimension of color in so many things is a recent phenomenon. Life itself was, in those days, not excessively colorful. The sneakers of my youth did not come in bright rainbow hues. Electric lime green and purple were to be found nowhere in my wardrobe, and certainly not in that of the adults I knew. Pink, bright yellow and orange did not contaminate the serious business of retail store signage. As a rule, buildings did not dare stray far from the colors of concrete and brick. The orange roof of Howard Johnson's restaurants was so exceptional that the roof alone, in fact, became its colorful trademark.

Appliances like refrigerators and washing machines came only in white, telephones and typewriters only in black. Even after black was no longer the only color of choice for automobiles, black remained America's preference. My grandfather's 1941 Oldsmobile was considered very modern because of its smart, two-tone color scheme—light gray and dark gray.

Bright and dazzling was, for the most part, reserved for Christmas, Halloween, and a few children's books. Color had its place in the world, but it was not in the serious business of real life. It was reserved for places like toy stores, the Sunday comics, and Hawaii. Television, newspapers and most magazines existed without the added dimension of color. Even Life Magazine depicted much of life itself in black and white. Most of the color between its covers was in the form of advertisements, ironically, the only part of the publication that did not portray real life.

It never occurred to me that the tiny black and white television in my parents' living room displayed only an unrealistic representation of what I was watching. Those early cowboys of TV westerns would have looked jarringly out of place had their gray surroundings suddenly taken on the hues of real life. The gray landscapes of prairies and western towns would have looked cartooney had the sky become suddenly bright blue with beautiful greenery all around. As a kid, I had seen enough family albums to know that life in the early 1900s did not happen in color. It was a monochromatic world. The dust-covered towns of the old west were supposed to be gray. Their storefronts were not intended to be painted in a colorful spectrum of hues, or their saloons to have bright, colorful signage and wallpaper.

Cartoons, on the other hand, were an entirely different situation. The cartoon characters that popped out of comic books and the Sunday paper were not attempting to represent real life. Somehow, Lil Abner, Popeye, and Donald Duck had always lived a life of color. Tweety Bird was born a bright yellow, Woody Woodpecker vivid shades of red and blue, and Porky Pig a bright pink. And although Mickey Mouse was born black and white, he wore bright red shorts and big yellow shoes to compensate.

The colorization of my monochromatic world happened gradually. It was the brave few who first realized that driving a bright red car would not make them look like cartoon characters. A multi-colored wardrobe would not make them seem like ridiculous clowns, although I do recall a few notable exceptions to this. By the early 1960s, it was commonplace to see color beginning to permeate all aspects of life. Television programs, magazines, and eventually the perpetually-drab newspapers all joined the new, vivid world. Even kitchen appliances such as refrigerators dropped their familiar white in favor of trendy, new gold and avocado green options.

By the time I graduated from high school, color was everywhere. Black and white was suddenly associated with old fashioned. Family photos now displayed an endless parade of flashy neckties and gaudy dresses.

Perhaps that's why I still enjoy looking at the old black and white family photos. Maybe it's because the colors I imagine in those worn and faded prints are not overly cheesy. I imagine the clothing is dignified and in good taste. The overcoats, fedora hats, slacks, and jackets seen as various shades of gray in the old photos I imagine are not dissimilar from how they appeared in reality. Even women's purses and high heels were always black. Family members are portrayed as the distinguished people I'm proud to have descended from.

When I look at the album of glossy, colorful drugstore photos that came years later, I am reminded of the questionable styles of the 1960s and 70s. I can't block out that purple, batik sports coat I wore to the school dance. Nor can I un-see my Dad's Bermuda shorts that scream out in flamboyant shades of turquoise and orange.

I guess I will always have an affinity for those old, gray memories that allow me to use the crayons of my imagination to color inside the lines. And with apologies to my grandparents for re-imagining their gray Oldsmobile a shiny bright red, I will continue to re-paint the distant past in the most colorful way possible.

On the Road

The 1950s saw a vast network of highways open the country to intrepid travelers intent on seeing firsthand the beauty and vastness of America. My father took this new system of interstate roadways as a sign that he should build a covered wagon for the family so that we might head out and begin to explore. Our travels would not consist simply of a few jaunts around the neighborhood, but as he insisted, a lengthy journey all the way to Florida and back from our home in Massachusetts.

Now before you get the wrong idea, the covered wagon he was intent on building would not be pulled by some overworked horse needing to be fed and rested every five miles. It would instead be towed by our much more powerful, albeit less reliable, 1941 Plymouth. The wheels would not be the old clackety-clack wooden-spoked relics seen in all the cowboy TV shows of the day, but actual tires. An arched canvas top would provide sufficient height to allow storage of all the items necessary for such an ambitious voyage, and wide enough to serve as the family's sleeping quarters each night.

Hearing no resistance from my mother, and only enthusiastic encouragement from us three kids, he set about building his wheeled ark. After careful measurements and design, but with no garage in which to work during winter months, construction of the frame began in our kitchen. When the project reached the stage at which getting a bottle of milk from the refrigerator required navigating a life-threatening obstacle course, the project was moved outside. This, however, meant disassembling the construction in order to reassemble it out in the driveway.

After months of hard work, the covered wagon was ready to be attached to the old Plymouth to see if it would actually withstand the rigors of the road. A successful trial run meant our journey was now all but assured and fast becoming a reality. Mom began gathering piles of clothing and kitchen equipment in preparation for the long journey while Dad assembled a series of paper road maps acquired free from our local Esso gas station—the kind that, once unfolded, could never be refolded to their original configuration.

Finally the day came when our long trek was underway. One after another, each unwieldy road map was in turn, exchanged for the next in the series that would eventually lead us into the deep south. Dad had preplanned and highlighted the network of roads to be followed based on sights we might choose to see on the way and cities to avoid due to the possibility of heavy traffic. No one wants to see a covered wagon attempting to navigate the busy streets of New York City.

As a young boy, I was enthralled by the varied terrain we traversed on our journey. And the old Plymouth did a masterful job of lugging our arched-roof, wheeled bedroom through it all, though there were times when the limits of the old car were glaringly evident. The ups and downs of Virginia's Blue Ridge Mountains taxed the poor engine to its limit. When the rains inevitably came, the ancient windshield wipers felt the strain and came to a complete stop. This, Dad explained, occurred as a result of the wipers drawing all their power from the vacuum of the engine itself. On the upside of the steep hills it was asking enough of the old car to power its way to the top, but apparently asking too much to be able to actually see where we were going.

Driving through South Carolina in the 1950s I saw things that did not exist back home in our New England states. During a gas station stop I asked Mom about a drinking fountain that featured a sign reading "Whites Only." I remember how difficult it was for her to provide a suitable answer that did not provoke additional questions on my behalf. We were certainly entering a different world.

Other memories that stand out are trivial, but made an impression on my young mind simply because they were different from what we were used to. The Spanish moss hanging in long strands from trees in Georgia, the different types of food advertised on billboards along southern highways, palm trees, the Luray Caverns, and the vast fields of cotton all made a lasting impression on my northern sensibility as did the occasional warnings of possible diamond-back rattlesnakes hiding in the bushes near where we stopped for a picnic lunch.

We finally made it to the Gulf coast of Florida where we stayed for several days before turning around and heading back to the ubiquitous scenery of Massachusetts with its familiar orange-roofed Howard Johnson restaurants and colonial houses.

Although this would be the only trip on which the family would haul our homemade covered wagon, more trips were to follow during which we would camp along the way to yet other distant destinations. In preparation for the first of such road trips following our southern journey, we had retired our old Plymouth in favor of a newer, though still used, 1955 Ford Ranch Wagon. This provided better viewing of the passing countryside through its many windows and by making use of its fold-down rear seats, one could actually stretch out and nap while traveling through boring sections of the trip. (My apologies to Ohio.)

Our trip to Michigan also saw the first use of our brand new twelve-foot square camping tent. This too was a considerable upgrade from our previous sleeping quarters, as I could walk right in through a handy zippered flap under a nice awning. It was tall enough so that, once inside, I could actually stand, although had I been older than nine, this might not have been possible. The assembly of our tent was a somewhat lengthy procedure, not to mention inconvenient if it happened to be raining. Eventually, the tent was upgraded to a camping trailer and, although this again had to be pulled by a car, we also upgraded to a 1961 Chevy station wagon to do the heavy lifting. After stopping at a campsite for the night, our new camping trailer converted almost instantly into a pop-up tent simply by pulling each end of the trailer outward. Not only was the camping trailer a huge time-saver, but it comfortably slept our whole family which had now grown to Dad, Mom, and four kids. There was even room enough for me to bring my guitar for sing-alongs after dinner.

My dad made what the family referred to as the "camping kitchen" that sat atop the roof of our car. Made from two huge slabs of plywood, it featured hinged doors that swung open on each side to accommodate pots and pans, canned goods, bread and peanut butter, a propane stove, utensils, fishing poles, and anything else that wouldn't fit in the car.

Our new portable motel now made it possible to make even longer trips to more far-away places. Our California trip was an epic voyage that took us to the beautiful west coast via the fabled Route 66 through Oklahoma, Texas, and New Mexico, stopping to take in various sights along the way. We lingered long enough in Arizona to hike the Grand Canyon, carrying enough water to get us all the way to the very bottom. On the steep trail down, we were passed by people riding mules and carrying sleeping bags and other provisions. Seeing that we were not weighed down with backpacks and other equipment, they commented on how brave we were to attempt such a trek on our own and so empty handed. Unfortunately, no one told us that having arrived at the depths of the canyon, there would be no Dunkin' Donuts at which to refill our canteens. The long and more arduous hike back up to the canyon rim took nearly the rest of the day and ended on wobbly legs with all of us panting like dogs in a sauna.

We finally made it all the way to the coast of California by taking this southern route through deserts and the salt flats of Utah. After visiting San Francisco and other attractions, we headed back to Massachusetts via a more northern route that took us through Washington, Idaho, the Dakotas and even part of Canada. While traveling through the mountains of Montana, the discomfort caused by my sister striking me on the back of my head with a snowball was mitigated by the sheer joy of being able to actually make snowballs in the middle of August.

It was at a campground during this return trip that we encountered swarms of mosquitoes so thick that it was nearly impossible to get out of the car. My mother, however, braved the elements in order to prepare dinner for us, and having decided to leave the security of our vehicle in order to eat at the campsite's picnic table, we constantly swatted as we ate. Our meal, however, was interrupted by a loud noise that sounded like a jet airplane driving through the narrow dirt roads of the campground. It was the welcome sight of a mosquito fogger machine in whose path was left giant clouds of poison repellent that descended over the entire campground adding a distinct flavor to our macaroni and cheese even as we attempted to shield our plates. We finished our meal ingesting insect poison by the mouthful and endangering our very lives with every bite. But at least they weren't mosquito bites.

It's the Little Things that Matter

Imagine for a moment that our sun is the size of the period at the end of this sentence. Were that the case, you would need a microscope to see the earth, and our entire solar system would fit on the page you currently hold in your hand. Our galaxy, in the same scale model however, would be the size of the entire continental United States. If you're not feeling small enough yet, consider the fact that there are more than one hundred billion galaxies in the known universe.

When I first heard these statistics, I thought to myself, *"Why am I obsessing about ironing all the wrinkles out of my pants?* Does it really matter if there are weeds in my lawn, a scrach on the fender of my car, or if my Internet is slow? And why should anyone really care if I just misspelled the word scratch in the previous sentence?

For that matter, why should anyone care who wins an election, a war, or the World Series? Why should anything that happens on this tiny spec of a planet make one bit of difference to any thing or anyone. The duration of any creature that has ever lived on earth is limited to an insignificant fraction of time on the most insignificant spec of real estate in the cosmos.

When put in a universal perspective, the things we obsess about begin to seem trivial and insignificant. The price of gasoline will have no effect on our minuscule planet as it hurdles through space at a speed of sixty-six thousand miles per hour. And the earth will keep spinning regardless of whether or not the pyramids are crumbling, the stock market is down, or that I spilled juice on the sofa.

If we are such insignificant beings clinging to this microscopic spec of dust flying through space, why then do we seem so important to ourselves? Why do we feel that every decision we make, every action we take makes any difference to anyone or any thing? Our decision whether to buy the gray sedan or the sporty red convertible will have no lasting impact on what we call the universe. Yet, at the time, it seems to be all that matters. Whether we graduate from Harvard and become a doctor or drop out of high school to become a dishwasher at Bob's Burger Bar will have no lasting effect on the world. Yet it seems to have an importance that actually defines the totality of our very being.

The fact is, our awareness cannot even begin to comprehend the vastness of all that is. For that reason, our only option is to live our lives on a scale we can understand. Suddenly, it's the little things that matter. The tiny fish swimming in a small pond has no awareness that anything exists above the surface of its watery world. It has no concept that there exists anything beyond the limits of its everyday experience. All of its attention goes to finding a meal and avoiding becoming one.

Similarly, our universe becomes one of tiny objects, events, decisions, and circumstances that effect our everyday lives. We focus on those things over which we have some control, or at least some understanding. In doing so, the little things then become large. The little things become all that matters. Everything we do, say, build, destroy, eat, and look at takes on a totality that becomes our universe.

When I was ten years old, I remember seeing a mosquito land on my arm. My first impulse was to slap it before it could bite. But I hesitated. In a rare childhood moment of deep thought, I paused and wondered if the tiny insect also had thoughts. And if so, what did it think about? How far did it believe its world extended? Was it aware there were other insects on other parts of the planet? Did it even know it was on a planet? Or did its awareness extend only as far as my backyard? And as I reached back to slap the tiny insect I wondered if its tiny insect friends would notice its absence.

The uncharacteristic pause lasted only a moment. As I slapped the pesky insect out of existence I pondered the fact that in one brief swat I was able to bring an abrupt end to an entire life, minuscule though it was. As I wiped the smear off my arm, it occurred to me that the life I had just ended may have seemed minuscule only in my own mind. To the mosquito, it was the totality of its consciousness. It was its universe.

Similarly, there will be those who wonder about what lies beyond our own experience. Are there some giant beings that look down upon our world and see us as fish in a tiny pond? Are they so distant and completely out of scale to us that we may never be aware of their existence? Could there come a time when one of them notices the tiny spec that is our world and, without even a thought, swats our entire universe out of existence like a annoying mosquito?

Until this unlikely event happens, or until the day a giant meteor unexpectedly collides with earth and destroys all we've ever known, it will be the little things that disrupt our universe. It will be the thunderstorm that causes a power failure, or the nail that causes a flat tire. It will be the bathroom faucet that won't stop dripping, or perhaps the fact that the coffee shop ran out of blueberry muffins that disrupts our lives.

But I digress. Enough of this bleak, doomsday nonsense. Now if you'll excuse me, I have to finish ironing my pants.

Walking on Water

It's not that I've always had a biblical desire to walk on water. But when the opportunity presented itself, I thought, "What would Jesus do?"

The year was 1980, and I decided to practice this unlikely feat for several days on a small lake in rural Maine. The lake was of such small proportion that its designation as a lake was questionable. Its opposite shore could be reached in a row boat within twenty minutes. Quaint family cottages dotted its perimeter sporadically, and from the small dock at the camp where we were staying one could walk several yards into the shallow lake before the water touched the bottom of your bathing suit. Now, however, I was preparing for a miraculous stunt that would see me walk considerably beyond that point while barely getting my feet wet.

My initial attempts proved comical to all observers as my family watched me from the comfort of their lounge chairs on the sandy shore. Arms flailing, but failing to keep my balance, one try after another ended in a plunge into the clear and shallow lake. I did not, however, view these short-lived attempts at walking on water as complete failures. Landing in the beautiful, refreshing lake was not without its benefits, and I usually gave in to the temptation to remain submerged and enjoy swimming around for a while.

This walking on water thing was proving to be not as easy as it seems in the Bible. Undiscouraged, I repeated my attempts at water-walking until finally I was able to remain upright on the surface of the water and walk with a remarkable degree of stability.

This drew amazement and applause from my family of spectators still watching in awe from the shore. A few swam out to where I was stepping across the watery surface to get a closer look and to ask if I would teach them my new-found talent.

Okay, here's the part I haven't told you yet. My seemingly miraculous performance was not one of supernatural powers. The contributing factor that made this miracle possible was a novel invention consisting of two large styrofoam floats with indentations into which you place your feet. The oversize pieces of styrofoam were large enough to support the weight of an average size adult human and capable of being maneuvered, providing you could maintain your balance. Once mastered, walking in a straight line was easy enough. Turning and changing direction, however, proved more difficult, but a necessary function if you didn't want to find yourself unavoidably intruding on the private camps bordering the opposite shore.

Every such walk always began either by stepping out onto the water from the very edge of the sandy shore, or by stepping down onto the water from the dock. Either way, the walk was begun in a standing position which, hopefully, would be maintained for the duration. Once balance was lost and you splashed into the lake, getting back up was next to impossible. Perhaps with a lot of practice, this maneuver might have been possible, but I was a novice who was just getting my feet wet, so to speak.

The more I practiced, the more confident I became at water-walking, and I was even able to help a couple family members achieve the same degree of proficiency. Boaters from neighboring camps did double-takes as they repeatedly circled the area to witness this strange phenomenon. The residual wakes created by the boats often made my continual upright posture challenging, but it was all good practice at maintaining balance. By the time our week at the family cottage was nearing its end, I felt my skill at this odd activity had improved to the point of near mastery. Nearby swimmers in my vicinity and kids jumping off the community raft posed no hindrance. Even passing boats literally did not upset me.

Now I was ready to take the show on the road. Upon hearing of my new skill, Jack, the head of the Public Relations department at the company where I worked thought it would be a brilliant idea to stage an event on the banks of the Charles River in Boston. The plan was for me to embark on a shore-to-shore walk while photographers documented the event and cheering onlookers applauded. The appropriate media outlets would be notified, and it would be billed as the first non-winter walk in history across the famous river. At the time, the Charles was widely viewed as a contaminated body of water, so Jack cleverly had the foresight to recruit a nurse who would stage a tetanus shot for the cameras upon the successful completion of my walk. Ultimately, scouting trips to the river determined that the currents were too much of a deterrent for a safe crossing. In the end, the head of the company refused to allow the agency to be associated with the publicity stunt and plans were scrapped.

Later that summer, however, I took my styrofoam "feet" to Concord, Massachusetts and the shores of Walden Pond, made famous by nineteenth-century poet, Henry David Thoreau. As I stood on the beach eying the vast surface of placid water stretching out in front of me, I noticed a lone fisherman sitting in a rowboat a considerable distance off-shore. Confident now of my skills at traversing wide expanses of water, I decided to pay him an unexpected visit. Although he sat quite a long way from the beach where I stood, I could see that he appeared to be facing away from me toward the opposite shore. My visit would indeed be a surprise and I imagined myself slowly walking up behind the man and caus-ing him to nearly fall out of his boat in shock. I'd be laughing so hard that it might prove difficult to remain upright on my buoyant footwear, but I ultimately decided it would be worth it to see his astonished reaction.

With that, I took a deep breath and set out across the surface of Walden Pond with excited anticipation of my jaw-dropping visit. As I approached, I was glad to see that the fisherman still had his back to me ensuring that my visit would, indeed, be a surprise. Forward progress being what it was for such a ponderous means of transportation, it took quite a while before I found myself in his vicinity. Nearing his loca-tion, I began to rehearse what I would say when he turned in amazement to see someone casually walking up to him on the surface of the lake. I would be as nonchalant as possible, acting as if this were a normal, everyday occurrence. Then I'd wait for his astonished reaction. I just hoped he didn't have a heart condition.

Finally I was within several feet of the rowboat and the fisherman still remained unaware of my presence. Although I tried to be as silent as possible, it was difficult to avoid a few light splashing sounds as I plodded one foot in front of the other. Luckily, a continuous series of small ripples hitting the side of his wooden boat produced the same splashing sounds and he didn't seem to notice anything out of the ordinary. Now was the time to make my move. I decided to interrupt the splashing of my footsteps with the unexpected sound of my voice. Anticipating a startled reaction, while at the same time, trying not to scare him, I would simply ask the most mundane question I could think of and wait for his shocked response after dropping his fishing pole and falling over backwards in the boat.

"Catch anything?" I finally asked casually.

I waited. After what seemed like several seconds of perfect silence, the man calmly turned his head without so much as blinking.

"Not much," he calmly responded. "They're just not biting today."

Now I was the one who was shocked. How could anyone witnessing a grown man standing on the surface of the water, having apparently walked across the lake to get there, not be in awe? How could anyone not be shocked and startled at the sight? But nothing—no double-take, no jaw-dropping wide-eyed stare. Not even a grin of acknowledgment.

My surprise attack having failed, we exchanged a few

benign comments and I turned to begin my disappointed retreat. My walk back to the beach seemed much longer than the walk out. Maybe I was just tired. Perhaps the letdown drained the excitement from me. At any rate, it gave me a chance to think, to ponder. I went into a state of relaxation until joy gradually overcame my discontent. The light and playful splashing of my feet suddenly became cause for blissful happiness and I continued the remainder of my walk in peace.

Still, I wondered how the fisherman could have been so blatant in his deadpan response. How could he not have had the common courtesy to give me the slightest indication that he appreciated my extreme efforts to provide him with a great story to tell his wife.

Again, I thought to myself, "What would Jesus do?" So I decided to forgive the arrogant bastard.

Disturbed Individuals

Then there was the time I discovered a dead body at McDonald's. Oh, it wasn't slumped over a happy meal at a table in the dining room. It wasn't even inside the restaurant. It was, however, just outside only a few steps from the parking lot. Jonathan Spelling, whose body lay just steps from the side door drew little, if any, attention from the steady stream of customers intent on the promise of a Big Mac and fries. No notice was taken by the happy children gleefully skipping from their parents' cars. Patrons waiting at the drive-through window seemed unaware that they had just passed within feet of a lifeless corpse.

Further investigation revealed that Jonathan's body had undoubtedly been there for quite some time—one hundred and seventy-two years, to be exact. According to the slate head-stone protruding above the grass next to the parking lot, Jonathan Spelling died in 1842, long before McDonald's ever sold its first hamburger. He lies next to several of his family members who had assumed that their final resting place in back of the Spelling farm would always be one of quiet repose. Over the centuries, however, the spot has transitioned from the tranquility of a remote corner of their property to the unceremonious bustle of a commercial fast-food establishment. So, instead of close proximity to the pearly gates, the unsuspecting Spelling family now finds themselves lying at the foot of the golden arches.

Here in New England, thousands of individuals lie in what used to be quiet and undisturbed private burial plots. Today, however, many of these sacred resting places are encroached on by municipal thoroughfares, urban sprawl, and overrun by an onslaught of public indifference. Many are now adjacent to the commotion of shopping centers and the din of interstate highways. One exit ramp off Route 95 in York, Maine passes so close to a family plot that one can almost read the inscriptions on the six headstones as you exit the highway.

Another small family cemetery in my neighboring town of Newington, New Hampshire is located at a strip mall just steps away from the entrance to what is now "Party City."

When I explored the tiny Pickering family cemetery, I counted nine family members whose remains yet inhabit this tiny plot. Back in the 1860s when the last of the Pickerings was laid to rest here, the family could not have imagined that a century and a half later countless people would still visit this hallowed ground. Nor could they have imagined, however, that the vast majority of those visitors would be coming to buy party favors and balloons.

Although it is quite rare these days to be laid to rest adjacent to one's former dwelling place, it remains legal in most states. As long as the proper paperwork is filed with the city or town and all regulations are followed, it is possible to keep Uncle Harry right out back. You don't even need a casket. As long as your loved one is covered with at least three feet of earth, and kept at least one hundred feet from the house, he's welcome to stay as long as you want. The law also states that Uncle Harry should be kept at least one hundred feet from any school. This has nothing to do with the restraining order placed on him after that "playground incident." It's simply the reverse of the regulation that prevents schools from being built too close to an existing cemetery. School children hate it when dead people show up next to the jungle gym.

Rare though it is to be buried today on family property, generations ago it was common for family members to be interred within sight of the family dwelling. As decades passed, however, family farms were sold, sub-divided, or otherwise lost to the original owners, and with them, the remains of their previous inhabitants.

Forty minutes south on a particularly commercialized section of Route One in Massachusetts, the Douty family lies directly at the entrance to a gas station. When the Doutys were buried here beginning in 1816, the automobile had yet to be invented. There were no noisy motorcars clattering their way in to refuel. If, indeed, the roadway existed at that time, it would have been a narrow dirt trail with wagon wheel ruts. The most intrusive thing those early Doutys would have endured would have been the occasional stray horse unceremoniously relieving itself on the ground directly above them. Now, as they look down upon the sight of the endless line of cars practically rolling over their graves, the Doutys must be rolling over *in* their graves.

So blatantly obvious are the Douty headstones, that few customers could possibly miss the out of place markers that rise upward from the sacred ground. Yet as their car is being refueled, few take the time to walk a few steps to read the names of those who had just welcomed them to their gas station.

Fortunately however, not all individuals interred in private family plots have been so blatantly overrun by the intrusive footprints of modern civilization. On an outing to the John Greenleaf Whittier house in Haverhill, Massachusetts, the curator escorted me around the main house pointing out some of the highlights of the property. Being a historic landmark, the homestead has not been subjected to the desecration of commercial sprawl. Unlike other ancient family estates, it retains the quiet charm cherished by its original occupants. It remains, in fact, a well-preserved estate in an idyllic setting. Aside from the asphalt paving and telephone poles along the approach road, it is not difficult to imagine what the estate must have looked like when it was built by Thomas Whittier in 1688.

The curator then directed me to the family burial plot at

the rear of the property and I climbed the small rise in back of the farmhouse to have a look. Thomas, the original occupant, and his wife, Mary, who journeyed to America in 1630, lie next to each other, undisturbed, along with several generations of their descendants. The tidy little plot remains much the same as it was centuries ago. Upon my return the curator told me of a recent elementary school field trip to the property. He had led the students up to the family burial site informing them that for generations this was where all the heads of the family were buried. One third-grader upon hearing this, stared at him wide-eyed until he eventually summoned the courage to bashfully ask, "Where's the rest of them buried?"

Such well preserved family plots, however, are the exception. Most individuals interred in private cemeteries have not escaped the onslaught of public intrusion. Whether it's a McDonald's, a gas station, or a strip mall, the continued encroachment into these tranquil grave sites is inevitable. As suburbs continue to grow and shopping centers continue to expand, family cemeteries will continue to be overrun and squeezed into the cramped corners of public thoroughfares.

Some may view the intrusion of urban sprawl into the quiet domain of long-deceased residents as a blatant infringement of sacred ground. But there's another way to look at it. Without the constant inroads into these tiny cemeteries, the ancient remnants of these former families would no doubt become overgrown ruins and totally forgotten. The fact that there is a Starbucks or a Burger King pushing its way up to a grave site preserves at least some public awareness of what would otherwise be shrouded in the wilderness of dark forests. The Doutys, the Spellings, the Pickerings, and countless other families would be lost to the elements and to all but, perhaps, a few local historians.

As long as these family plots remain in the path of the passing public, they will also remain in the context of public awareness. There will continue to be the anonymous citizens who pluck the weeds, trim the shrubs, and straighten tilting headstones. And there will always be those few kind souls who check for litter on their way back in for another cup of coffee.

While some long-passed individuals still remain within earshot of commercialism, still other sleeping souls have been unlucky enough to find themselves too close to its inevitable onslaught. Indeed, some have been deemed to lie so inconveniently close to the perils of industrial advancement that they have actually been forced to get up and move. When I worked in Boston, I would occasionally walk past a mass grave tucked away unobtrusively in a corner of the Boston Common. It is here that an unknown number of anonymous people have been redeposited into their new home.

This alternate resting place became necessary in 1895 when excavation for America's first subway system discovered these unfortunate individuals who had brazenly and inconveniently taken up valuable space exactly where the Park Street subway station was to be located. No one could have imagined the scale to which this trove of human remains continued to pile up as the dangerous work of digging the subterranean tunnels continued for years. Estimates are that between 900 and 1,000 bodies were unearthed during excavation.

A single headstone now commemorates the jumbled cluster of remains. The memories of those who lie crowded below are now remembered in just a few chiseled words: "Here were re-interred the remains of persons found under the Boylston Street mall during the digging of the subway. 1895."

It is believed that the resulting mass grave may contain casualties of the battle of Bunker Hill as well as British soldiers who perished during the siege of Boston in 1775. It is also thought that because of the unmarked nature of the original graves, there may also reside herein the bodies of former undesirables such as murderers, thieves, pirates, military deserters, native Americans, Quakers, and witches. No longer in separate apartments, however, they now find themselves living not as strangers, but as roommates in one massive hole next to the Boylston Street entrance to the subway.

So to all those individuals so rudely disturbed and subjected to the unrelenting advancement of modern life, I offer my apologies on behalf of the entire world. And to them I say rest in peace. Sort of.

Holy Pizza

The minister was only a couple minutes into his Sunday morning sermon when a man in a Domino's Pizza uniform balancing a large pizza box with one hand burst through the door at the back of the sanctuary.

"Someone here order a pizza?" he called out.

Aghast, the entire congregation, mouths open and eyebrows raised, turned in unison to witness in disbelief the brazen assault on their pious sanctity. Seeing nearly one hundred of his faithful followers glaring at the intruder and two men seated in the back row about to forcibly remove the unwelcome visitor, Minister Tomkinson immediately took steps to quell the situation. From his pulpit, he calmly asked the gathering if anyone had indeed ordered a pizza. Faced with deafening silence, he then politely addressed the pizza delivery man.

"Uhhh... I think you must be in the wrong place."

Lifting the order form taped to the top of the pizza box, the intruder hesitantly read from the slip of paper.

"Is this... 54 River Road?"

"Yes it is," replied the minister. "But you're clearly in the wrong place. There are other businesses in this building.

Perhaps you should try one of those."

Now in Pizza Man's defense, Unity Church in South Portland, Maine looked nothing like your typical church. In fact, it looked like an ordinary office building at the far end of a parking lot. There was no steeple, no stained glass windows. The building itself was a rather plain structure and was, in fact, home to several businesses.

Becoming suddenly aware that he was interrupting a rather large and now hostile looking gathering, Pizza Man looked around timidly and began to slowly retreat toward the door through which he had so abruptly intruded. As he neared the far end of the center aisle, he apologetically held up one hand.

"I'm sorry. I didn't realize... I didn't know you were having a meeting."

The minister again sought to assure him that there were no hard feelings.

"That's okay. I was just beginning my sermon."

"Sermon!" exclaimed Pizza Man who, looking around, had now halted his retreat. "Is this... Is this like a church or something like that?" he asked.

The minister quietly nodded and replied with a grin, "Yeah, something like that."

"I'm sorry. I didn't see a steeple or anything," he said as if to justify his mistaken assumption. "Is this one of those low-budget churches?"

Chuckling, Minister Tomkinson replied, "Well, we consider ourselves rich in other ways."

Pizza Man looked around, grinned knowingly, and nodded. "This is one of those *cults*, isn't it."

"No. This is Unity of Greater Portland," assured the minister, now attempting to engage the young delivery man.

"And this is a *church*?" queried Pizza Man.

"That's right. A *Unity* church."

Pizza Man, looking around again, pressed the issue. "I don't see any statues of Jesus. No crosses. You know, Jesus on the cross?"

"Here at Unity, we identify more with love and light," replied the minister. "Not so much the death and torture part."

"I don't know," countered the young man sceptically, now seemingly inclined to continue the conversation. "The church I used to go to was full of that stuff. Crosses everywhere, a big altar, pulpit, people in robes all over the place, a great big pipe organ. I think you need all that stuff to be a *real* church."

"I assure you, we're a real church," replied the minister. "And you don't need all that stuff to know God. We believe God is inside every one of us."

"*Inside* you!? Are you sure this isn't a cult?"

"No, it's not a cult. We worship God here. And we follow the teachings of Jesus. Here at Unity we try to understand what Jesus was really saying, and we try to be more Christlike ourselves."

After a long pause through squinted eyes, Pizza man finally asked, "Does God know you're doing this?"

"We certainly hope so," offered the minister. "Here at Unity, we take to heart the essence of what Jesus was saying and leave a lot of the rest. You know, the stuff that was invented later by the so-called men of the church."

Pizza Man continued warily, "I don't know. You'd never

get away with that where *I* used to go to church. They don't sell pizza by the slice. You have to take the whole thing or nothing at all. Ya gotta take it with the works. Ha, ha. get it? *The works.* A little pizza humor there."

"Yeah, yeah, I get it," the minister grudgingly conceded. "By the way, what's your name?"

"Uhhh... John," he stammered. "John Smith."

"John, I notice you said where you *used to go* to church. You don't go anymore?"

"I kinda got out of the habit," replied Pizza Man. "It just wasn't doin' it for me."

"Well, John," continued the minister. "You're welcome to join us for the rest of the service if you'd like."

Pizza Man did not immediately respond, but looked around at the gathering of congregants who were still attempting to come to grips with what was happening.

Okay... confession time. The man in the pizza uniform? That was *me*. And the banter in which I was engaging with the minister was an elaborate hoax concocted by the two of us and performed to an unsuspecting congregation on an otherwise typical Sunday morning. It had been my contention that with the large number of relatively new congregants, there may have been some who still were not entirely familiar with the principles of Unity Church. Under the charade of explaining this to me masquerading as a pizza delivery man, new members of the congregation would vicariously learn the basics of this spiritual community and how it differed from basic religions.

When I presented my unorthodox idea to Minister Tomkinson along with a script, I didn't know exactly what to expect. I had anticipated at least some hesitation as he weighed the possible backlash to such an outlandish prank. My relief came with a bit of surprise when he immediately smiled and said, "Let's do it!"

After a couple rehearsals, I visited a local Domino's Pizza restaurant to ask if I could borrow a uniform for a few days. After explaining my idea and assuring them that I would not wear it while making fake pizza deliveries or robbing a bank, the manager passed a uniform to me over the counter. He handed me an empty pizza box adding, "You'll probably need one of these too." Again, the lack of resistance to my plan was somewhat surprising as demonstrated by the ease with which I was able to obtain the necessary props for my undercover operation.

Several minutes into our skit, and following the minister's offer to join the congregation, I took a seat near the front of the sanctuary. As I carefully placed my pizza box beside me, people finally began to realize the whole thing had been planned. Smiles gradually replaced their jaw-dropping expressions. The two "bouncers" at the back of the sanctuary quietly returned to their seats. For the remainder of our "performance" the congregation was not only entertained, but even long-time congregants learned more about the spiritual principles that were the foundation of Unity as the minister, under the guise of explaining to Pizza man, provided a basic overview of its beliefs and practices.

As the sermon concluded, Minister Tomkinson introduced me, adding that I was a regular attendee at a Unity church in the neighboring state of New Hampshire, and that I did not actually work at Domino's. I stood to acknowledge the polite, but reluctant applause as the choir began their final selection.

As the last notes of the choir faded away, the gathering moved to an adjoining room where refreshments were served. A crowd of mostly friendly church-goers crowded around me, though some seemed disappointed that I did not actually come bearing pizza. Though years have now passed, the memory of my sudden visit remains vivid. The event was to go into the annals of church history as the day when a pizza delivery man came not to deliver a pizza, but to deliver a sermon.

A Growing Appreciation
for Weeds

I kneeled in a posture quite suited, I thought, to weeding or praying. Today I was doing both. Uprooting the stubborn sprouts one by one and praying they wouldn't return. In front of me, my pathetic little grouping of petunias grudgingly summoned forth a few feeble blossoms in acknowledgement of my countless hours of attention. I systematically scanned the soil, painstakingly stripping it of unwelcome weeds. I repeated, trance-like, the quick, efficient rhythm. *Reach, pluck, toss. Reach, pluck, toss.* Having been programmed to its repetitive mission, my arm now continued the process on its own, leaving my mind free to pursue daydreams induced by the warm sun on my back.

I suspect several minutes had passed when my attention was redirected to the end of my outstretched arm. There, pinched between my thumb and finger was a perfectly healthy weed which moments before had been thriving in the shadow of what I hoped would prove to be zinnias. I drew it to my face for closer inspection. Barely two inches tall, it was well-proportioned with a healthy root structure, and already showed signs of tiny, perfectly formed yellow buds. Yet I had uprooted it like an unwelcome squatter in deference to a less vigorous, albeit, more "cultured" hybrid.

It was a moment of profound clarity which I now find somewhat difficult to recreate. I squeezed my eyes closed in a prolonged blink attempting to dismiss the thought as absurd. *Too much squatting in the hot sun,* I thought, as I flicked the specimen onto the wilted layer which now covered the bottom of a cardboard wine carton over three inches deep. I continued in a more deliberate manner with renewed enthusiasm. *Reach, pluck, toss.* My fingers, however, had barely begun to seek out the next intruder when my rhythm was halted by the absurd irony. I stopped, mid-reach, blurting out loud, "Huh..?"

The sound of my own voice made me vaguely aware of where I was, and I looked around to make sure none of my neighbors had seen me talking to myself.

What caught my eye instead were dandelions. Dozens of their brash little heads rising above an otherwise adequate lawn. The damp denim of my jeans clung briefly to my knees as I rose to my feet and surveyed what lay before me. I acknowledged an inner smile, though I doubt my face ever betrayed my traitorous thoughts. The coarse, yellow petals now shown in a totally new light. I felt as if I were looking at them for the very first time. They looked somehow... *different.* In the full sunlight, their bright yellow blossoms were suddenly transformed into a cheerful scattering of happy faces.

What I saw at that moment was not a condemned and despised nuisance, but rather an entire kingdom of overlooked, under-appreciated plants thriving among vegetation which, for some reason, we consider more desirable. What could be more desirable in a plant than the ability to adapt and persevere in the face of the most adverse conditions? We uproot them. We poison them. We pluck them from their beds with barely a thought. Still they manifest in profuse abundance against the cutting jabs of trowel blades and selective plant genocide. The irony was palpable, and again I found myself uttering aloud, "What the Hell?"

Why is it, I thought, that we spend so much time coaxing the very plants that are reluctant to perform, while we discourage those that do so magnificently even without our help? What is this need we humans have to control nature in an unnatural way? Maybe it's just that. The need to control. After all, if we let things grow in natural order as they wished, the result would be total garden anarchy. Complete and utter disorder. Rarely content, however, to be passive observers of nature, we assert our superiority as a species by changing the very nature of nature. Could it be that perhaps it is only our mindset that needs changing?

My attention was jolted back to reality by the sound of my neighbor's garage door lifting. Larry, a balding stockbroker, and non-gardener, leaned over the fence with a big grin at the sight of my weed box.

"They'll just grow back, ya know."

"I know... Damned weeds!" I added the latter descriptor in an attempt to cover up my sudden misguided affinity for them.

Larry headed back toward the garage to retrieve a shiny set of golf clubs unaware that weeds weren't the only thing growing just over the fence. A conspiracy was quietly, yet undeniably taking root. And it threatened to overturn the entire hierarchy of my garden. Over the next week or so, the seeds of this blasphemy lay waiting to sprout and blossom into a fully-formed insurgency.

The dictionary defines "weed" simply as "any plant that grows where it is not wanted." Not content, however, to rely on such oversimplification, I consulted the head of a local agricultural school for further insight, only to discover that he concurred with Webster's brief classification. In the apparent absence of any botanical distinction, the classification seems to be based totally on horticultural snobbery.

Dandelions, in fact, are of the very same family as sunflowers, and every part of them is edible. Up until the 1800's, dandelions were seen as extremely beneficial, and people actually removed grass in order to plant them. A cup of dandelion greens, in fact, contains 535% of your daily recommended amount of vitamin K and 112% of vitamin A.

Now, I'm not suggesting that I have no appreciation of the cultivated hybrids which abound in the perfect gardens of well-tended suburbs. Even in my own garden, the modest results of cultivation can be seen holding court in the late spring around my birdbath. The ruffled gowns of bearded Iris, and my colorful collection of exotic Lilies are testament to the rewards of tampering with the natural order of things. Nor do I pretend to be a gardener's gardener. I don't know the Latin names of what I plant, and I'll probably always confuse Gaillardia with Gazania.

But wasn't it today's seasoned gardeners who, as children, held to their lips dandelions gone to seed, and watched as their breath cast featherlike seeds drifting to out-of-sight meadows and backyards? Even the most ardent among us were full of innocent wonder before we learned to condemn.

Could there still be a place in our hearts, as there is in nature, for the shunned specimens which collectively we have judged worthy of such a disdainful label? What if at long last we were able to see the perfect beauty in what we have stepped on and uprooted for so long? It may not always be an outer beauty, but they possess qualities perhaps in some ways, more deserving of our admiration.

The tolerance I am suggesting may seem misguided at first. Even blasphemous. And I'm certainly not advocating a hands-off policy which would relinquish our beds to the chaotic jumble which would surely follow. What I am suggesting is that we reconsider our judgement and need for total control over nature. That we humble ourselves to consider the possibility that those little plants that appear almost overnight between our tidy, cultivated rows deserve a place in our hearts, dare I say, in our gardens.

It might begin in a small way. A quiet shift of consciousness in a forgotten garden corner. Call it an exercise in allowing. A trial reconciliation with weeds. However you justify it, you'll be secure in the knowledge that should this new relationship not work out, you have not allowed anything of lasting consequence. At any time you are free to renew your personal commitment to the extermination of any plant you deem offensive. At best, you'll have developed a tolerance for a part of nature formerly associated only with toil and frustration. You will have kindled a new sense of freedom when you realize to your surprise that occasionally when taking the time to "stop and smell the roses," you, instead, find yourself "appreciating the weeds."

When you can find a place in your heart, as there is in

nature, for these shunned specimens, you find that something unexpected happens. They grow on you.

I Do

Judy walked into my office with a serious look on her face and closed the door behind her. *Uh oh,* I thought to myself. *She's going to give her notice.*

Judy was one of my best employees, a diligent worker who was loved by everyone. I'd hate to lose her. She then approached and sat down in the chair opposite me, never once taking her eyes off mine.

"I have something very important I need to ask you," she began.

My worst fears all but confirmed, I prepared myself for what she was about to say, at the same time wondering how much I would have to offer her to stay. She leaned toward me, her eyes still fixed on mine, as she opened her mouth tentatively to speak.

"Will you marry me?"

Completely taken aback, I was at a loss for words. I began to laugh as I studied her face for some sign that this was all a joke that one of the other employees had put her up to. Showing no hint of levity, however, she waited patiently for my response. I leaned back in my chair in a subtle attempt to distance myself from her space which was suddenly becoming slightly uncomfortable.

"Well," I began, with a slight chuckle. "I'm very flattered, but I'm already married."

Now it was Judy who laughed. "No," she countered. "Will you marry *me and John?*"

Now I was thoroughly puzzled. "How can I do that?" I stumbled. "I'm not a minister or Justice of the... I'm not anything."

Judy held up both palms in my direction in an attempt to stifle my confusion. "I've looked into it and all you need to do is get a certificate from the Governor to become a commissioner of civil marriage."

"What?" I queried.

"Yeah. There's an application you'd have to complete, and personal references you'd need to supply. But I'm sure it wouldn't be any barrier for you. I mean you don't have an arrest record that I know of, and there's nothing that would prevent you from qualifying... That is, unless you don't want to do it."

"No... I mean Yes! I mean I'd be happy to marry you. I mean marry you and John that is." I began to wonder if my stumbling over my own words was now causing her to have second thoughts about her request.

Judy explained that, as her boss, I had been a positive force in her life and had demonstrated the type of inspiration and creativity they had been looking for in the person who would perform their wedding ceremony. Neither she nor John being particularly religious, wanted someone who could compose a beautiful speech and preside over a memorable ceremony that their families would look back on with fondness.

A week or so later, applications and requirements for my one-day "solemnization" license completed, it was now time to prepare for the big day. The wedding was to take place in the shadow of Harvard University on the banks of the Cambridge side of the Charles River where the couple had first met. What to say, I wondered. Everyone would be watching me and expecting some inspiring words to commemorate such an important event. A bit of history first, I thought, to engage the attendees. After all, the river that separates Boston and Cambridge had been the backdrop of many historic events throughout many generations. Besides, I rationalized, if they had wanted someone to just quote Bible verses or poetry, they would have chosen someone else.

The day arrived faster than I could have imagined. Judy and John, dressed in their wedding attire, now stood before me in the presence of their families and friends. I glanced down at my notes and cleared my throat as I began what I hoped would not be a bumbling performance by their non-minister officiator. After welcoming the guests, I began by establishing the context of the location in which we found ourselves.

"The ground on which we stand today," I began, "has been witness to a rich and varied history. Since the 1630s—well over three-hundred years ago—this very spot has felt the footsteps of the founders of our country, and the literary, scholastic, and artistic genius of this and past centuries."

I took a deep breath and wondered if I should not have prepared a few Bible verses just in case.

"But for Judy and John," I continued, "this will no longer be simply the place where, in 1775, General George Washington established headquarters and surveyed the encampment of his troops."

Having not shared my speech with the about-to-be new-lyweds ahead of time, I studied their faces in an attempt to discern any sign of disappointment in the direction my oratory was taking. Seeing only anticipatory smiles, I continued with my history lesson.

"It will no longer be merely the ground on which Longfellow sat as he formulated words which still endure today. This will no longer be just a riverbank on which were spent the idle hours of T. S. Eliot and Winslow Homer. The very spot on which we stand today will no longer be commemorated only as the place where John F. Kennedy strolled between classes at Harvard."

I paused to allow the gathering to feel the significance of the very spot on which we stood. I also wanted to make sure there were no frowns on the faces of those who were still expecting those Bible verses. Seeing none, I proceeded.

"For Judy and John, however, this spot is about to take on a much more historic significance. For Judy and John, this is about to become the place where they made a commitment to join their two lives."

The rest of the speech went off without a hitch. The couple shared vows. They exchanged rings. After I pronounced them married, everyone gathered at a nearby hotel in Harvard Square for dinner and dancing.

It would not, however, be the only time I would be recruited to become a marriage commissioner for a day. Some years later, my niece in California asked if I would officiate her wedding. Being an old pro, I agreed without hesitation.

Feeling emboldened by my initial foray into officiating, and the fact that I was now in front of my own family, I began the ceremony with a declaration to not only stress the importance of the occasion, but to set a tone that I knew my family would appreciate.

"Welcome to this celebration of love and commitment," I announced. "An occasion so joyous and momentous that, for many of us, it happens only two or three times a lifetime."

Knowing my own family, they laughed appropriately. Understanding, however, that the occasion was not a venue for stand-up comedy, I quickly settled into a serious ceremony. As was the case at Judy and John's wedding, my speech was heartfelt and hopefully received with love and sincerity. Following the beautiful outdoor ceremony, we all assembled at tables on the lawn for food, drinks, and music. As was also the case following Judy and John's wedding, all that remained was for me to now make it official by filing the signed paperwork with the city clerk's office.

One of these days I'll get around to doing that.

Lack of Imagination

I've been aware for quite some time that New Hampshire, the state in which I reside, has several towns and cities with the same name as those in our neighboring state of Massachusetts. A little research on my part revealed an astonishing result. The number of duplicate town names between the two states total a jaw-dropping sixty-eight.*

This is due to the fact that centuries ago as America was first being settled, colonists named these new settlements in nostalgic remembrance of those places, mostly in England, from which they had migrated. I get that.

In many cases, however, colonists traveled to the new world to escape persecution of religious and other freedoms as well as extreme poverty in many areas. So in the sixteen-hundreds when they settled the area around my home state, they faced the challenge of starting over and trying to forget the oppressive tyranny of the country from which they had fled.

"I say, Nathaniel, Now that we've finally escaped the insufferable oppression of bloody old England, we can finally put that misery behind us. Now we just need to name this place. How about New England?"

That I *don't* get.

Why would those early settlers want to name their new home as a tribute to the country from which they had just liberated themselves? Why would they want to be forever reminded of the tortuous monarchy whose tyranny drove them to embark on a death-defying voyage to an unknown world? Did those early settlers really lack what little imagination it would have taken to come up with a different name?

This lack of imagination would seem to be an inherent trait of their British heritage given that the boring succession of British monarchy goes something like King Henry the First, King Henry the Second, King Henry the Third, Henry the Forth, Henry the Fifth... You get the idea. Why should the names of their towns be any different? Why should they suddenly begin to demonstrate imagination?

While many of those early settlers were just too busy lacing up their waistcoats and breeches or eating Yorkshire pudding to waste time thinking of original town names, that was apparently no obstacle for the citizens of "Santa Claus, Georgia" or "Bread Loaf, Vermont." Nor did the inhabitants of "Friendship, Maine" and "Blue Ball, Delaware" have any trouble coming up with unique labels to prevent their towns from being confused with others.

And the citizens of "Buttzville, New Jersey" and "Truth-or-Consequences, New Mexico" also demonstrated their boundless imagination for municipal creativity. The latter, by the way, came about as a publicity gimmick when the radio game show "Truth or Consequences" offered to broadcast from any town that would name itself after the show.

I don't mean to cast aspersions on the early settlers of

this country whose bravery in crossing the Atlantic Ocean in primitive wooden boats was beyond belief. I do mean, however, that it might have been a good idea to bring a few more linguists over with them on the Mayflower.

Nor do I mean to single out my own state in this duplication of nomenclature. The realization that this phenomenon runs rampant across our entire country led me years ago to invent a game that I'd play with friends and family to relieve the boredom of long automobile trips. Sometimes we'd play simply to show off our knowledge of geography.

The object of the game is to visit as many states as possible by "traveling" from one to another by way of cities or towns with the same name. Here's the way it works.

Start in any state you want, and in any town within that state. Let's start, for example, in my neighboring town of Dover, New Hampshire. From there, we can go to Dover, Delaware. Once in a state, you are free to travel to any town within that same state. So let's go to Wilmington, Delaware, and from there to Wilmington, Massachusetts. Once in Massachusetts, we can travel to Salem, Massachusetts and from there to Salem, Oregon. In Oregon, we can travel to Portland, Oregon which allows us to travel to Portland, Maine.

At this point, we've already traveled to five different states. Now let's say we end up in a state with no way out. Let's say from Portland, Maine we go to Bethel, Maine, and then to Bethel, Alaska. Oops... dead end. Sure, we got to visit yet another state, but now there's no way out of Alaska. And that's the last place anyone wants to be stranded. That's why I added the backtrack rule which makes it perfectly acceptable to retrace your steps until you find yourself in a state from which you can choose another path on which to visit additional states.

Not only is this a great way to sharpen your memory and geography skills, but it's a great remedy for boredom when you have time to kill.

Who would have thought that the early settlers' unimaginative and boring use of duplicate town names would, four centuries later, become the antidote to boredom? Go figure.

*City and town names common to New Hampshire and Massachusetts: Amherst, Andover, Ashland, Auburn, Bedford, Belmont, Berlin, Bridgewater, Brookfield, Brookline, Chatham, Chester, Chesterfield, Concord, Conway, Dalton, Deerfield, Dover, Easton, Franklin, Goshen, Grafton, Greenfield, Groton, Hancock, Hanover, Haverhill, Hinsdale, Hopkinton, Hudson, Kingston, Lancaster, Lee, Lincoln, Littleton, Manchester, Marlborough, Merrimac,** Middleton, Milford, Milton, Monroe, Newbury, North Hampton,** Northfield, Orange, Pelham, Pembroke, Pittsfield, Plainfield, Plymouth, Randolph, Richmond, Rochester, Salem, Salisbury, Sandwich, Sharon, Shelburne, South Hampton,** Springfield, Wakefield, Walpole, Warren, Washington, Webster, Winchester, Windsor.

**Variations in spelling: Merrimac/Merrimack, North Hampton/Northampton, South Hampton/Southampton.

Food for Thought

An uncle on my mother's side, though educated at Harvard, extremely well-read, and culturally elite in many respects, was somewhat less so in his eating habits. I remember him reporting that on a trip to Germany, the first words out of his mouth in German were, "Ein Big Mac."

No matter how distant and foreign a destination, one will always be able to locate with little effort, a McDonald's, Burger King, Pizza Hut or Kentucky Fried Chicken. My question to those who would seek out these bastions of substandard dining in a foreign country would be *"Why?"*

It's bad enough here at home that you can't exit an interstate without running into the same ubiquitous golden arches and other familiar plastic monuments to culinary mediocrity. But now you can travel to the most exotic destinations and feel as if you've never left home.

The only place, in fact, to which I have ever traveled where America had not contributed to a gastronomic decline, was India. Because the cow is considered sacred in the Hindu religion, even Ronald McDonald would be labeled as blasphemous were he to attempt to sacrifice a cow for such a mundane ritual as lunch.

Other countries have apparently no objection, however, to our undermining their cultural traditions. So accepted is the American standard of questionable culinary taste, that when I visited Beijing, China, the world's largest McDonald's had just opened there. On opening day, forty thousand customers filled the restaurant's seven hundred seats while nearly one thousand employees kept the lines moving through the twenty-nine cash registers. The New York Times published a story in April of that year in which they quoted a Chinese college student named Zhang as saying, "It's a bit expensive to eat here at McDonald's. But I guess for a high-fashion restaurant like this, the prices are okay."

Not only had we contaminated their rich culinary heritage, but we had duped them into believing that this was America's idea of haute cuisine.

While laying no claim to being a snobbish food connoisseur, I have long held that one of the most interesting aspects of traveling is eating in ways that are not possible at home. Some of the most unusual and memorable eating experiences I've had have been in foreign countries.

One chilly night while still in Beijing, I went to an upscale restaurant (not McDonald's) with my sister's family. As we entered the establishment, we passed several vacant outdoor tables. Preferring to find seating inside where it was warmer, we continued into the dining room only to discover that the restaurant was filled to capacity. As we started to leave, the hostess approached us waving menus and insisting in broken English that she would find us seats. She beckoned us to follow as she headed back outdoors toward the patio seating area. My brother-in-law, John, who speaks fluent Chinese, began to explain that it was too cold to eat outdoors, and that we would find another restaurant. The hostess, however, kept walking, beckoning us to obediently follow. She walked past the vacant tables on the patio and out into the street. We looked at each other in perplexed amusement, shrugging our shoulders, but we politely followed, curious to see where this adventure would take us.

There had obviously been some misunderstanding. Between her broken English and John's Chinese she obviously thought we had said either "Hey, let's start a parade!" or "Please take us to the bus stop."

With dainty baby steps, she hurried down one street and onto the next, occasionally checking behind her to make sure we were still obediently following, while motioning to us that we should continue to do so. About a block away, she looked into another restaurant, and seeing that they had empty tables, led us in and gave us the menus she had carried with her on our long walk.

We hesitantly gave her our order, and the hostess scurried out the door and back down the street. Before long, a flurry of waiters, politely emerged from the chilly night air and presented us with the most succulent and splendid meals. They bowed slightly as they backed away and scurried out of the competitor's restaurant, as we were left to eat unmolested. Try that in America and see how fast you're back out on the street.

Another memorable dining experience in China was at a restaurant that served one thing only—duck. As I recall, there were three choices. Small, medium, and large. A choreographed team of servers worked with surgical precision as they masterfully dissected the bird before us displaying each component in the most artful manner. Every appendage, every organ, every succulent morsel of our duck occupied its own separate serving plate. Each part of the duck was served with elaborate fanfare, drizzled with its own special sauce, and presented in aesthetically pleasing arrangements although, as I discovered, there is precious little to eat on a duck's foot, and I was resigned to merely licking the sauce from it's webbed appendage.

In Australia, before I became a vegetarian, I found myself at one restaurant where patrons go into the kitchen and cook their own steaks. Elbow to elbow we stood as flames leapt up around our sizzling cuts of beef. I thought the audacity of this concept was genius. Not only is it a wonderful participatory experience, but patrons can't complain about how their steak is done.

Once in a while, the quality of food is overlooked in deference to the sheer experience of it. While strolling through an outdoor marketplace in Budapest, Hungary, my wife and I stumbled upon a most unusual dish. An enormous pan of large, acorn-size nuggets simmered in a red tomato sauce over an open flame. The aroma beckoned us for a closer look. As we neared the booth, the proprietor took one of the morsels on the end of a fork and proudly held it out to us for a taste. My wife tentatively took the fork as she read the sign above the pan: "Rooster Testicle Stew." As she slowly brought the fork to her mouth, I thought to myself, *thank God I'm now a vegetarian!*

There were places where I went out of my way to discover eating experiences unlike anything I might ever again encounter. On my return trip home from Australia, I stayed in

Tahiti for several days with a friend to unwind. Much of what you find to eat in the South Pacific consists of tropical fruit and seafood. One particular meal, however, stands apart from all others. In Papieté, the quaint seaport capital of Tahiti, a unique, nightly phenomenon occurs. Locals from the surrounding area drive their cars, pick-up trucks, and bicycles to park alongside the picturesque harbor. On their tailgates and the ground surrounding their vehicles, each family prepares its own specialty to be shared with friends and sold to tourists. Falling into the latter category, my friend and I walked the length of the docks, taking note of the different offerings of, perhaps, thirty families. One family was cooking some kind of meat on sticks, another, fresh fish on a grille. One man had the whole back of his pick-up filled with guavas and coconuts that he would cleave on demand with a huge knife and serve dripping with sweet juice. The meal we ate that evening came from about four different families, as I recall, each one providing one course. Fish from one vendor, vegetables from another, coconut milk shakes from yet another.

Sometimes it's not the food itself that makes a meal special, but rather the experience. That night sitting cross-legged on the docks of Papieté using our laps as tables, neither one of us spoke as we savored our four-course dinners that, all told, cost the equivalent of about six American dollars. Palm trees waved above us as the sun sank into the South Pacific, and in the silence, we each knew what the other was thinking. Restaurants don't get much better than this.

Out of My Mind

Well, it's happened again. Once again, I have failed to accomplish my end-of-year goal that I set annually with renewed hope. While I do not consider it an unattainable goal, circumstances largely beyond my control have continually dashed my hopes for success. Each year as the holiday season begins, I reaffirm with my deepest conviction that I will finally achieve a positive outcome. *This is the year,* I think to myself. *This is the year that I will finally make it through an entire holiday season without once hearing the song, "Have a Holly Jolly Christmas."*

My obsession is little more than a subconscious annoyance of which I am barely aware—until it happens. Hearing the song each year renews my desire to have *not* heard it. Of course, by then, it's too late. Then, I can't get it out of my mind. Some years I barely make it past Thanksgiving before the sound of Burl Ives' scraggly voice causes me to stop in my tracks. I puzzle at the song's nonsensical lyrics. I cringe at his decidedly non-musical inflections. For me, it's like fingernails scraping on a blackboard. Occasionally, I manage to get through much of December before the obnoxious discord is sprung on me as background music at the supermarket.

It's not that I don't enjoy Christmas music. I love Christmas music. There's nothing like good Christmas music to put you in that holiday spirit. I just don't like that particular song. Burl Ives sang the original version which is the one that is still played most on the radio. Now, I'm sure Burl Ives was a nice man. He even looked a little like Santa Claus. If only he hadn't sung that dreadful song. And if only he hadn't sung it so dreadfully. He recorded it decades ago, and I'm quite sure the man is now dead. Unfortunately, his recording lives on.

It's not that the song itself is any worse than some of the other cheesy pre-holiday drivel that contaminates the airwaves. The thing that makes this particular song so irritating is that, for some reason, it sticks in my mind, and I find myself humming it incessantly. Turning the radio off doesn't help. All it takes is a few notes to plant the irksome melody firmly in my head. Once started, it goes on for days like an endless loop. When this happens I have certain remedies on which I rely to dispel the fixation. The problem is that they work only for a short period of time. I can recite the state capitals or hum a brisk medley of Bee Gees tunes for only so long before that, too, gets on my nerves. I find myself hoping for a distraction of some sort. A fire at the mall, a purse-snatching incident in which I race after the culprit and tackle him to the ground to the grateful cheers of onlooking holiday shoppers. In imagining both of these scenarios, however, I envision myself playing the hero while listening to *Have a Holly Jolly Christmas* being played over the mall sound system.

In a laughable twist of irony, I am now made acutely aware of the song by its very absence. I no longer have to actually hear the song for its nonsensical lyrics to plague me. I tentatively turn on the car radio and catch myself in silent prayer, *"Please don't let me hear it today."* In so doing, I have triggered the indelible tune that will demand my attention for the next few hours. I begin reciting state capitals again, and I am up to Nebraska before I realize that I have missed my exit.

The ultimate remedy, I suppose, has less to do with whether or not I hear the song, and more to do with my reaction to hearing it. So, this year, I have decided to employ a bold strategy. I have taken to deliberately humming the song while repeating the positive affirmation, *"Gosh, I love this song."* So far, it has resulted in only marginal success. The fact that I am hoping not to hear it is, in itself, causing me to think about it. Its very absence is enough to bring it to mind. And once brought to mind, there it remains, stubbornly planted in my subconscious.

I'm beginning to think that even if I never hear the song again, it will remain with me for the duration of my life. The one saving grace is that I am reminded of this curse only during the Christmas season. Once January arrives and the holidays are left behind, my mind moves on to the new year. I am now free to walk through the supermarket without hearing the irksome strains of *Holly Jolly Christmas*. Christmas music is now thankfully replaced by... Wait... Oh no! Is this that... *"Who Let the Dogs Out"* song?!

A Leap of Faith

Ground school was a mandatory prerequisite for jumping off the side of a mountain. Our small group of would-be hang gliders sat on the grass listening intently to our instructor, Jack, explain the mechanics and gymnastics necessary to defy the laws of physics. Balance and weight distribution, he impressed upon us, were key to allowing your attached wings to carry you through the air unaffected by the ceaseless efforts of some unseen force he called gravity. The bleak warning he offered, however, was still fresh in my mind as I climbed to the spot where I would tempt fate.

"There are two kinds of hang gliders," he announced to the class. "Those that have crashed, and those that *will* crash."

Not such encouraging words for those of us about to take a literal leap of faith. I still don't understand what those words were intended to instill in us, except perhaps, the fact that our unquestioning trust was about to be questioned. When does trust become gullibility? And who'll come rescue me when I'm up in the air yelling for help?

Aeolus Hang Gliding School in Massachusetts was the first such school in the country. Founded when the sport was still a novelty experienced by few, it drew people from the surrounding area who thought jumping off the top of a ski hill while harnessed into a metal frame with wings sounded like a good idea. We had been instructed to keep one arm positioned in front of the structural framework, the other behind it. This, as Jack explained, would prevent you from breaking your shoulder when you crashed. There he goes again with those comforting thoughts.

The name Aeolus is rooted in the distant past when only gods could fly. In Greek mythology, Aeolus was the keeper of the winds and King of the island of Aeolia. Classical writers regard him as a god who kept the violent storm winds locked safely away inside the cavernous interior of his isle, releasing them only at the command of greater gods to wreak devastation upon the world. Yikes! Had he been talking with Jack? Hopefully, on this beautiful summer day, the gods would be silent and let me crash in peace.

I don't recall how many times that day I climbed to the top of the ski slope, praying to Aeolus for a smooth flight before getting a running start and leaping trustingly into the air. I remember only that I did not crash, defying not only Aeolus, but also Jack's prediction of inevitable disastrous outcomes. A couple students in my class did indeed have less than smooth landings that day, but I don't recall injuries of any sort, and no ambulances were called to the sight.

To be clear, this was not some rocky precipice high up in the Alps we were leaping from while thumbing our nose at Aeolus. The landscape beneath our airborne and prone bodies was a steep, though gently rolling ski slope. During the winter months, it was covered with snow and joyful skiers flying downhill trying not to break their ankles. During the off-season, it was home to a handful of excited hang gliders with the same objective. A nice, grassy carpet of green was there to soften our landing and, thankfully, would not show the blood nearly as much as snow.

As it happened, I did not find myself at Aeolus Hang Gliding School about to partake in this questionable activity because of a lifelong dream to risk my neck. I had not been obsessed with heights or enthralled by the sight of daredevils in the sky with little visible means of remaining there. My participation came about as a result of having created a brochure and other promotional materials for the owner of the company. When he offered to enroll me in the class for free, I figured what's the worst that could happen? Not thinking through the answer to my rhetorical question, I jumped at the chance (figuratively speaking) and immediately signed up.

You're probably thinking I was about to say, "Big mistake!" But you'd be wrong. Not only was ground school interesting and informative, but standing at the top of the ski slope about to launch myself into the air, I was struck with how secure I felt having just learned the mechanics of safe flight. The only regret I had was that I had not brought a film crew with me to record the event.

Before our initial leap into mid air, we were given last-minute reminders about shoulder position and balance. I say we were given "last-minute reminders" and not "last rights," although where we would end up was still in question. Watching the ground fall away beneath me I remember thinking, "Okay, that was the easy part." I did not dwell, however, on how or where I would land. The exhilaration of using my own wings to overcome gravity was all I could think about. So much so, that I have no recollection of landing. I must have at some point, however, touched down because I'm sitting here years later writing this account.

After several flights, our small group gathered at the base of the ski hill to compare experiences. As it turned out, my very first flight was enough to earn me a certificate indicating that I had flown farther in a hang glider than the Wright Brothers had flown on their first flight at Kitty Hawk, North Carolina. My initial foray into flying through the air with my own wings remains, if you'll pardon the pun, a high point in my experience. To this day, the certificate remains on my wall as a reminder, not of the length of my flight, but of the pitifully brief duration of Wilbur and Orville's initial attempt in an airplane. Subsequent Wright Brothers' flights not only attested to their perseverance, but led to an entire aviation industry with a man on the moon a mere sixty-six years later. As for me, I decided to quit while I was ahead. (And still alive.)

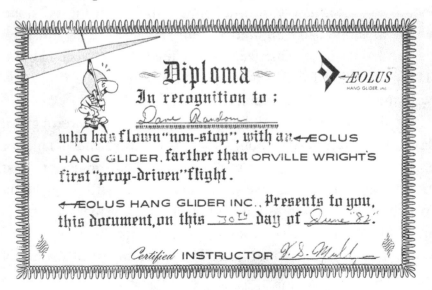

It's Complicated

Waiting to order my coffee, I let out an exasperated sigh as the line had not moved for at least five minutes. I turned to the couple standing behind me and impatiently rolled my eyes upon hearing the woman in front of me order what I considered to be only slightly less complicated than the nuclear codes.

"A double-tall, half-decaf pumpkin-spice turmeric latté with two shots please."

Just as the barista turned to either prepare the concoction or perhaps consult a chemist, the woman added, "Oh, and with oat-milk foam."

The couple behind me acknowledged my perplexed look and shrugged upon overhearing this lengthy formulaic instructional. I thought to myself, *when did everything get so complicated?* And *oat milk?* Even milk has somehow become complicated. Oat milk, soy milk, almond milk, coconut milk, rice milk. I wouldn't be surprised someday to find that some crazy entrepreneur has managed to squeeze milk from a cow.

In the food category alone, there are so many choices, so many decisions to be made. When I was a kid and the family went out to dinner, we were never approached and asked if we'd like to hear the gluten-free and vegan specials. And no one ever asked if we had a nut allergy.

Food is a good example of something that, over the years, has become more complicated. It wasn't that long ago that you didn't have to decide whether you wanted regular, organic or free-range poultry. Chicken was chicken. No one cared if the chickens were kept in a chicken coop or if they were allowed to run around in the yard playing hide and seek. There was no such thing as grass-fed beef. And farm-raised salmon was never an option.

Even water, the most basic substance to human life, is not exempt from this trend of complexity. When I was growing up, we drank water right from the tap in the kitchen (and occasionally from the garden hose). We didn't think about whether or not there was rust or lead in the pipes leading into our house. Having lived through that apparently life-threatening era, we now buy water at the supermarket in a staggering array of choices. There's mineral water, distilled water, sparkling water, flavored water, artesian water, reverse osmosis water, and spring water. But not just any spring water. You then have a choice of Alpine spring water, volcanic spring water, naturally effervescent spring water. If my ancestors could see how much we happily pay for a small bottle of this stuff that comprises more than seventy percent of the earth's surface and pours out of the sky for free, they'd turn over in their graves. Then they'd have a nice drink of water and go back to sleep.

There's a store about five minutes from my house that sells salt. That's it, just salt. But, unlike the big blue Morton's Salt containers my mother used to buy at the grocery store when I was a kid, this salt comes in tiny glass jars and is available in over fifty different flavor infusions like Sriracha-Infused Sea Salt, Bolivian Pink Artisan Salt, Chardonnay Oak Smoked Salt, and Icelandic Volcanic Lava Sea Salt to name just a few. So now you have a choice. But no longer can you just say "Pass the salt please." Now you have to be a little more specific.

Not to be outdone, a local chain of furniture stores offers ninety-one choices of mattresses. Even sleeping has now become complicated. Every night as I lay down on my Sleep Number mattress, programmable to my exact comfort level with separate controls for each side, I think about my distant ancestors who were happy to have a bed of hay to lay on that was dry and not contaminated with crawling insects.

Now, I'm not saying these overly-complex choices are a bad thing. We can handle it. It's great that we have so many variations and choices in our everyday products. I'm not complaining. I'm simply marveling at how the world has changed. As society becomes more sophisticated, consumers have become more discerning in what they choose to buy. It seems no product is immune to these overly complex variations.

My wife is a biker—a *serious* biker. And, like her biker friends, she has more than one bike (each purchased at an astonishingly high price). No longer content to pedal around on just any old bike, these serious, multi-bike pedalers select which of their many means of transport they will ride out on based on their specific ride. They have road bikes, gravel bikes, mountain bikes, racing bikes, touring bikes. Then, depending on the time of year, tires are adapted as seasonal conditions dictate. No biker in her right mind would be caught riding around on winter tires in the middle of August. Not only would that confirm to her biker friends her ignorance of proper equipment, but also her ignorance of, I don't know... what month it is?

The other day I went to put a load of laundry in the washer and was confronted with so many different settings that, for a moment, I was completely bewildered. Now, I'm no stranger to doing laundry. But I'm so used to running the washer on whatever setting has been pre-selected that I don't even look at the dials. I just throw the clothes in and hit "go." But because my mind has lately been noticing things that tend to be complicated, I happened to notice the vast array of multiple choice questions and was at a loss to make an informed decision. Normal, heavy duty, deep steam, quick wash, delicates, permanent press, sanitize, allergen, extra rinse, high spin, medium spin, low spin, no spin, extra spin, spin only, steam, cool water, warm water, hot water, extra hot water.

After completing that test, there's an extra-credit question about soil level if you're feeling up to the challenge— light, normal, or heavy. I stood baffled with my arms full of a week's worth of clothing and studied the machine's dashboard as if for the first time. Suddenly the aroma of my worn T-shirts rose up to greet me. I threw the load in, closed the door, and hit "heavy."

Again I thought of my ancestors who, if they were lucky enough to have anything resembling a washer that wasn't powered by hand, there was probably just one setting— "wash." After the simple process that followed, the heavy, wet laundry was put through a wringer and hung on a clothesline in the backyard. Two days later the clothes were ready to be ironed. What a simple world it was.

The Cold Hard Truth

Every winter people sing of beautiful, white snow-flakes gently floating down and glistening in the lane. We've all heard the familiar lyrics: *a beautiful sight, we're happy tonight, walking in a winter wonderland.*

I don't know who wrote the song, but chances are, he was an employee of the New England Board of Tourism. He was, no doubt, hired to entice more prospective tourists to head north for a nice, quiet winter holiday and to spend money at local shops while enjoying the beautiful, white snowflakes fluttering to the ground. Many unsuspecting travelers actually believe the misleading claims invoked by the popular song, and envisioned by those who sing its sweet melody. Most singers of this classic winter carol, however, only know the opening lyrics. They never get to the third or fourth verse. So in case you missed the disclaimer at the end of the song, here's the fine print:

Not all winter precipitation comes in the form of wispy, white snowflakes that float gently to the ground. Results may vary. Past performance is no guarantee of future results. Views expressed in this song are solely those of the song writer and do not necessarily reflect those of any individuals who may be referred to in the lyrics. Carolers who choose to repeat these lyrics while singing should recognize the words they sing as wishful thinking and not necessarily based on fact. Any opinions relayed in said song are for illustrative purposes only and should be viewed as such. Side effects may include varying degrees of chill, temporary lack of feeling in feet, fingers, or other bodily extremities. If this should happen, seek immediate shelter indoors under a warm blanket and drink plenty of warm liquids. Winter tourists hereby agree to take complete responsibility for any possible risk factors, including injury or death caused by slipping on ice or being buried alive by snow plows. New England makes no warranties of any kind with respect to expectations based on song lyrics as written or implied by its writers who may or may not have ever visited New England in winter. Any offensive language overheard by tourists while passing residents who are shoveling snow or attempting to scrape ice from car windshields is entirely the consequence of unforeseen circumstances, and while we understand their frustration, this shall not be seen as an endorsement of their opinions. Appearance of any white snow is subject to change once it has been on the ground for longer than one hour. Do not come to New England in the winter if you are susceptible to bitter cold, slippery ice, or any form of slush. New England or any portion thereof shall not be held liable for any discomfort or disappointment suffered by the user.

Now don't get me wrong. I don't hate winter. It's the ice, the snow, and the cold that I hate. For those who ski, ice skate, or snowshoe, it may very well be seen as a winter wonderland full of pristine ski slopes and snow-laden wooded valleys. Indeed, winter travelers come from great distances to partake of New England's White Mountains and beautiful hiking trails.

In recent years, however, shoveling snow has become my only winter sport. It's not so bad when the snow is light and fluffy, but when it's wet and heavy, I sometimes feel like I'm shoveling mashed potatoes. I watch my shovel bend under its gravy-laden payload as I lug one shovelful at a time from my driveway and deposit it nearby with all the grace of an elephant falling down the stairs.

Occasionally I pass the time by absentmindedly counting each shovelful. By the time I get to about three hundred or so, I'm ready to call it quits and take a break. If the snowfall is a prolonged event, clearing the driveway may be done in two or three stages as it's often easier to clear six inches at a time rather than wait for total accumulation and attempt to remove fifteen inches of the white stuff in one outing.

Often, however, when I bundle up and go back out for a second or third round, I discover that the snowplow has come by and formed a rock-hard and dense crusty retaining wall of icy snow at the end of the driveway. Because this snow has been compacted by the weight of a giant metal blade forced upon it by a three-hundred and fifty horsepower truck, this formation is usually heavier even than what I had been previously shoveling.

By the time all traces of winter excrement have been removed from my driveway, it's finally time to once again head back inside. Now I am able to take full advantage of the comforting warmth of the living room sofa, and I enjoy it while I can. Tomorrow's forecast calls for snow.

As winter progresses, it's residual effects are left as a blight on my otherwise beautiful hometown. The occasional snowman stands guard over front lawns as evidence of happy little kids who have yet to be charged with shoveling duty. But most of what is left behind by winter weather does not conjure up idyllic, picturesque postcard scenes. It takes almost no time at all for newly-fallen snow to turn into an ugly, sloppy mess. Densely congealed piles of slop line every street, forming blackened, dirt-encrusted barriers which are fondly remembered in the lyrics of absolutely no songs. As passing cars splatter sidewalks with wet, salty brown slush, caked and hardened footprints become icy, treacherous landmines lying in wait to take unsuspecting pedestrians down with them. Gigantic piles of snow the size of small houses are dumped into the corners of Walmart parking lots and left as blatant reminders that sometimes last until late April. All this is compounded by the fact that it's pitch black by four-thirty in the afternoon. Winter is certainly nothing to sing about.

While snowfall may indeed occur sometimes as delicate, feathery flakes such as those written about in nostalgic songs, the characteristics of snow is entirely dependent on weather conditions at the time. More often than not, winter storms are wet. Often, this snow is accompanied by gusty winds that bring down tree limbs and power lines leaving residents in the dark. If you happen to be outdoors during one of these snow events trying to extricate your car out from under three feet of heavy white slop, the punishing winds can whip the snow into a horizontal blizzard of tiny ice pellets that sting your frozen face like hundreds of bee stings. Even as you turn your back to the frigid winds, you find that your eyelashes have frozen together and your glasses have fogged up. By the time you finally manage to free your car from under the shapeless mound of snow on the side of the street, you discover that, not only can you no longer feel your fingers, but it was actually your neighbor's car you've been working to uncover the whole time.

So when you sing those happy winter songs about fluffy white snowflakes fluttering down and Jack Frost cheerfully nipping at your nose, remember to do a reality check. That fluffy white snow can sometimes seem to weigh nearly as much as wet concrete, and it usually doesn't stay white for long.

And Jack Frost? Well, let's just remember that he was named after the word "frostbite," a severe condition that freezes bodily extremities like fingers and toes, and is responsible for dozens of amputations each winter. But don't let me discourage you from visiting New England in the middle of our frigid cold winter. Keep singing those deceiving winter ballads. And as you sing those sweet, heartfelt lyrics, don't say you weren't warmed. I mean *warned*.

Look on the Bright Side

I've always been an optimist. Whenever someone asks me whether I'm a "glass half empty" or a "glass half full" kind of guy, my answer has always been the same. I'm a "glass is overflowing" kind of guy. I always look for the good in everything. So when a friend was unceremoniously dumped by his girlfriend after he had just bought her an expensive necklace, I told him to look on the bright side. There's always a silver lining. I told him it could have been worse.

He stared at me as if I did not understand what he was going through. "We've been together for five years and I thought she was the one. How could this have been worse?" he asked.

Having not thought ahead for an appropriate comeback, I gave him the most empathetic look I could muster and replied off the cuff, "Well, she could have been dating your best friend." He continued to stare at me with an expression that could best be described as incredulous. The brief conversation ended when he finally replied, "*You're* my best friend."

Now, I'm not suggesting that my friend's failed relationship was a cause for celebration, but there are some people who just find it difficult to find any good in a bad situation. And, I'll admit there are certainly those situations in which it is difficult to see that any good could come of it. Sometimes the silver lining is hard to see, and it may take a while to show up. Some people, however, seem to have a knack for always finding it, no matter how hidden it lies amidst the negative aspects of an event.

In a world where both positive and negative may exist simultaneously, there are many situations that seem to encompass both ends of the spectrum, and even good news is sometimes tempered with bad. I've learned that when someone presents a good news/bad news scenario, the bad news often seems at first to outweigh the good, so I'm always ready for the other shoe to drop. Usually, when a positive and upbeat situation is presented immediately followed by a "but," I brace myself for a letdown. However, being an staunch optimist, I am more inclined to look for the good in any situation that first presents itself as bad.

Leo Arthur Kelmenson, the head of the New York-based ad agency for which I worked was an optimist of the highest order. If he couldn't immediately see the good side of a situation, he'd create one. Such was the case on the day we learned we had just lost our largest account—The Ford Motor Company. Not only was Ford an account that brought in hundreds of millions of dollars to the agency each year and paid the salaries of many of our high-paid employees, it was also a highly visible account with much esteem.

When Mr. Kelmenson requested that the employees of all of our many branch offices gather to listen in on an agency-wide conference call, we knew something big was happening.

You don't summon hundreds of employees across the country together to announce a new copy machine. I sensed that today's announcement might be one of those "good news/bad news" kind of scenarios.

My instincts were not unfounded. Mr. Kelmenson first thanked everyone for taking the time to listen in on his telephone broadcast. Then he dove right in by announcing the big news. The collective gasp that followed threatened to suck all the air out of the conference room in the Boston office where I happened to be. This was certainly one of those situations, I thought, in which there would be no silver lining, no bright side. But what Mr. Kelmenson said next both surprised and amazed me.

"This puts us in a great position," he continued in a surprisingly upbeat tone. "We are now free to go after the Chrysler account." Six months later we were doing all of Chrysler's advertising.

The year was 1980. Chrysler had just received a controversial government bailout to save it from bankruptcy. At the time, it was the largest rescue package ever granted by the government to an American corporation. It seemed an improbable scenario with a very questionable outcome. No one knew if Chrysler would even survive. Half a year later, however, we were working with Chrysler's CEO, Lee Iacocca, as his company became our new largest account. Chrysler's resurrection was one of the most successful economic comeback stories in American history and it was our agency that helped bring it back from the brink of disaster.

It was, for me, yet another reminder that when one door closes, another one opens. Sometimes "plan B" turns out to be better than one could even imagine. We've all had it happen. Like the time I discovered that great restaurant only as a result of taking the wrong highway exit and getting lost. And I never would have ended up in the perfect campground site had my first choice that summer not already been taken. Nor would I have found that two-million-dollar winning lottery ticket in the hospital parking lot had I not gone to the emergency room after getting my foot stuck in a watering can. Okay, that one never happened. But you get the idea.

Sometimes the silver lining might be small. Occasionally, however, it can be life changing. I started my own successful business only because my former employer closed the regional office where I worked. At the time, I was devastated. But it worked out better than my wildest dreams. We're constantly presented with opportunities to look on the bright side.

A colleague of mine was scheduled to make an important presentation to a gathering of business leaders at a financial conference. Alex would be showing off his presentation skills to Mr. Mahoney, the Senior Vice President of our company who was considering him for a promotion to department head. Knowing that a successful presentation would justify his promotion, his nervousness was beginning to show.

The stakes were high because also among the group of business leaders were several executives of an insurance company we hoped to gain as a client. This would be their first impression of our agency, and what would hopefully justify their signing on with us. In a way, this was Alex's audition to both the prospective client as well as the boss.

After his introduction, Alex gathered his stack of papers and rushed up to the podium probably a little too quickly. As he attempted to organize his notes in front of him, his sleeve caught on the corner of the podium and one page of notes fell to the floor. Slightly embarrassed, he went to retrieve it. In doing so, he tripped on the microphone cord and the entire stack of papers flew off the podium in disarray.

As he attempted to catch some in mid-air, the microphone also toppled to the floor with an amplified thud complete with audio feedback. Flustered, he rushed to gather his scattered papers and the scene quickly began to unfold in a comedy of errors and successive mishaps.

Alex lifted one foot to unwrap the microphone cord now tangled around his ankle, and in so doing, lost his balance. He landed on the floor atop the blanket of loose papers as a few of the businessmen attempted to stifle their snickering. Alex quickly stood, aware that he was the center of attention, and straightened his suit jacket attempting to regain his composure.

I sat at the back of the room along side our Senior Vice President who had started to shake his head in disbelief. Just when I thought (against my positive nature) that it couldn't get worse, Alex scrambled to gather the scattering of notes, but as he bent over to retrieve them, the back of his pants loudly ripped up the seam. By now, even the most stoic of the businessmen could no longer stifle their reactions, and the entire room erupted into raucous laughter. I looked to my left, and even Mr. Mahoney, hand to his head, was trying not to laugh.

Whether or not it had anything to do with Alex's presentation that day, we ultimately did not succeed in winning over a new client. While I don't remember the name of the insurance company we had hoped to impress, Alex's performance shall forever remain in my memory. I recall his embarrassment when word of his gaffs reached the rest of the agency. Disheartened and knowing my propensity for always looking on the bright side, he trudged into my office the next day looking for solace.

"I'm such a screw-up," he lamented, shaking his head. "I'll never live this down."

I put a reassuring hand on his shoulder not knowing exactly what to say. Finally, in an effort to provide some degree of comfort, I looked him in the eye and said, "Don't worry about it. It could have been worse."

Alex stared back at me in disbelief. "How could it possibly have been any worse?"

Again, at a loss for words, I took a deep breath and shrugged before answering.

"It could have been me."

CRAAAAP

Every once in a while as I'm going about my daily business, I like to imagine what it would be like for someone to accompany me. Not just anyone, but someone from a hundred or two hundred years ago. As I encounter modern inventions like cars and airplanes, or see someone on his cellphone pass me in the street, I try to imagine what my ancient companion would think about modern life. I enjoy the fantasy of imagining what it might be like if that person from a long-ago era could suddenly materialize and see these same things we take for granted. No doubt it would, for him, be beyond miraculous.

Today I was showing my imaginary nineteenth-century guest around the modern world as I did a few errands. He was confused, yet amused, at the simple conveniences to which we give barely a passing thought. A routine trip to the grocery store had him constantly shaking his head in disbelief. It began as we approached the store and the doors automatically opened to allow us entry. As we passed through, I imagined my guest turning back quizzically to see who had pulled the doors open and by what invisible means. Once inside, however, his attention was ripped from the mysterious ghostly doors to the overwhelming sight of what lay ahead. Aisle after aisle of products spread out before us in a landscape of unimaginable bounty. The staggering array of colorful packaging would have my companion gasping out loud.

In his day, purchasing dry goods and grocery items had been a quite different experience. Back then, stores were often no larger than a two-car garage. Customers would hand a shopping list to a clerk who stood behind the counter wearing a white apron. The clerk would then gather the items to be purchased, often reaching high up onto shelves using a long pole with a claw-like appendage on the end. One by one, the retrieved items were placed on the store counter until the list had been fulfilled.

It was, indeed, a very different world. Back then, the groundbreaking invention of photography was just beginning to open new possibilities. The tedious process of black and white images captured on glass negatives to be transferred onto paper was expensive, and therefore, not yet very common. Yet as I walked with him down the supermarket aisles, our gaze was met with hundreds of packages featuring the most colorful photographs. As we navigated the breakfast cereal aisle, he again made his presence in my mind known when he actually laughed out loud at the sight of colorful cartoon characters and beautiful photos of Cheerios with strawberries.

At the far end of the store, frozen foods were displayed in abundance without a single block of ice in sight. Exotic fruit like pineapples and Mangoes from far-away tropical islands appeared to have just been picked. Unthinkable luxuries pulled his attention from one to another as we passed. Items that had not yet been conceived, let alone invented had my guest hyperventilating. I had to explain to him that toilet paper was now used instead of pages torn from the colossal Sears catalogs that, in his day, lay ready beside virtually every commode waiting to be repurposed. Toilet paper, I explained, was now an everyday staple in every bathroom. I then found it necessary to further explain that bathrooms had now replaced the ubiquitous outhouses of his era. Around every corner, more and more unfamiliar items caught my guest's attention. He was amazed at every turn, and quite baffled at the sight of water for sale in bottles. All this waited within arm's reach to be placed easily into our self-service cart.

Of course, my guest was imaginary. I had conjured him up from the genealogy charts I so diligently work on from time to time. If it were possible to instantly blink a person back to life from say, a hundred and fifty years ago, he'd think he had just landed on another planet. I fantasize about being able to play host to that nineteenth century visitor, introducing him to our world of modern invention. Just an average citizen, a farmer perhaps, maybe a blacksmith.

Today I was playing host to my great, great grandfather, Henry Hermes. When Henry was born in 1840, there was no electricity. The automobile had yet to be invented. And flying through the air was the domain of science fiction. In the scheme of things, today's supermarket visit was a relatively tame experience. It was also very appropriate. You see, a century ago, Henry himself, had been the owner of a small grocery store at the corner of Cedar and Highland Streets in Roxbury, Massachusetts. My plan was to allow him to adjust to the modern world gradually. I decided the supermarket would be the perfect introduction.

When it came time to check out, Henry was again taken aback as the conveyor belt automatically moved our groceries to within easy reach of a young woman who passed each product over a tiny red light, causing it to emit a beeping sound. I inserted my plastic credit card into a slot on the small device in front of us. We were then allowed to carry our accumulated goods from the store without ever having to exchange any coins or paper money. I did not tell Henry how much the few bags of groceries actually cost or the process by which I would eventually be required to pay. Suffice it to say, that in the mid-eighteen hundreds such an amount would have allowed one to purchase several horses or, perhaps, a small house.

It would probably take a week or so for Henry to come to grips with the fact that all the laws of his nineteenth-century world had been upended. Thoughts of what was possible or impossible had been rendered obsolete, the laws of nature and physics rewritten. After another week, I thought, he might feel comfortable enough to agree to be strapped into a metal vehicle to careen down a super highway at fifty times faster than a horse-drawn wagon. Then, just as he'd be getting used to the blur of trees and other metal vehicles passing, I'd turn on the car radio. If he hadn't lost consciousness altogether from the shock of a distinctly human voice emanating from nowhere in particular, he'd wonder when this new language had taken effect.

When did everyone start talking in abbreviations? What happened to all the words? Why are people speaking in code? I imagined Henry in my mind furling his brow as he attempted to decipher meaningless strings of letters. People talking in abbreviations and acronyms had left him at a total loss for comprehension. Until he brought it to my attention, I hadn't realized how much we are now used to this new language form.

I tuned to the local public radio station. As the news was read, I became even more aware of how much we take for granted the constant barrage of non-words with which we now communicate. Today's news was about the aftermath of a hurricane. *FEMA* had been brought in to help the *EPA* at the request of the director of *HHS*. Turning to international news, the commentator reported on the *G12* summit and its proposed changes to *NATO,* the view of the *EU* on *BREXIT,* and how *NAFTA* might affect the *GDP* of the *US.* The station then paused for station identification. *"WBUR,* your local *NPR* station," the commentator announced, "at *103 point 9 FM.* And on the *Web* at *NHPR dot org."*

This new language had begun innocently enough. Back in the eighteen hundreds when people communicated only through handwritten letters, it was commonplace to find the occasional abbreviation interspersed among the perfectly penned cursive. The use of *"Mr."* and *"Mrs."* for example, was not only faster to write, but saved valuable ink when fountain pens had to be dipped into an inkwell after every few words. Initials of a person's name also became frequent shorthand. Other words were also abbreviated such as *"St."* to denote a biblical entity of high esteem, or *"lbs."* as in units of measure. But such shorthand was used only in writing. When speaking, the entire word in its original form was used. One still spoke of *"Mister"* and *"Missus,"* *"Saint"* Peter and five *"pounds."*

Today, our verbal communication is strewn with the remnants of what would otherwise be long, drawn-out phrases. Today, people are C.E.O.s, V.P.s, PhDs, C.P.A.s, M.V.P.s, YUPPIES, and LGBTQ. Companies are IBM, GE, and AT&T. Even Kentucky Fried Chicken is now KFC.

And the government isn't helping. With contractions like NASA, OSHA, NASDAC, the IRS, FBI, FDA, and CDC, it's a wonder there's no government agency whose mission it is to help people figure out what all these abbreviations and acronyms mean.

We enter our PINs into ATMs to get money ASAP from banks that are members of FDIC. We brag to the man at the DMV about how many MPGs our SUV gets. All this while we watch the NFL and NBA on our TVs.

My sudden awareness brought on by Henry's confusion was shedding new light on how we've corrupted our language. I tried to understand how it must feel to him hearing this unfamiliar vocabulary scattered throughout the language he grew up with. His native tongue must now sound totally foreign to him. The conversation continued in my head as he explained to me that back in the 1800s, literacy was not something to be taken for granted. Not all citizens were granted the privilege of an education.

"The English language was our common denominator—our *immutable constant*," he explained. "It was the one enduring underpinning that one could be assured would not be hijacked and pulled out from under us, even as the world around us changed. Our beautiful language," he complained, "now sounds like *crap!*"

He asked me if there was not some way this trend of

perversion could be reversed. I explained to him that something like that could not be just be legislated out of existence. I explained that the only possible way to slow the proliferation of such desecration might be to establish a peoples' movement through social media on the Internet.

"The Inter-*what?*" My time-traveling friend was now completely baffled.

"The Inter... Never mind," I said. "Tell you what... Let's come up with a catchy name and see if we can get people talking about it by posting it."

"Mail everyone a letter?" he queried.

"No, not that kind of posting. I'll show you."

After a few days of careful thought, I arrived at a suitable and brilliantly clever name for our peoples' movement designed to slow the growth of the verbal shorthand that pervades our sacred English language. One afternoon, I summoned Henry back into my mind, excited to share the results of my brainstorming.

"Okay, here goes," I said, anxious to hear his undoubtedly thrilled reaction to my idea. "Based on your recent comment that the English language now sounds like *crap*, we should call our new social movement "CRAAAAP." It stands for "Citizens Revolting Against Abbreviations And Anachronistic Phrases.""

Henry sat quietly unimpressed, failing to see the brilliant irony of my clever idea of using an acronym to stop the spread of acronyms. I sensed he was now glaring at me from his vantage point of one hundred and fifty years ago. Somehow, my humor had been lost over the vast expanse of time.

Finally, after a minute or so, his expression began to

soften. Then, with a smirk, I sensed his mood changing. I perceived a distinct feeling of pride being projected across the many decades that separated us. Finding himself suddenly on the leading edge of this contemporary and unfamiliar form of language, I felt his heart begin to swell. Henry had managed to propel himself forward in time to the point where he was now comfortably at the forefront of this strange vocabulary. Here was a unique, new word—an *acronym* if you will—in which he had shared authorship.

Feeling his comfort level increase, I made a promise to Henry. I agreed to continue to keep my mind open to his imagined thoughts. I promised I would be there to lead him as far as he dared go into the future. And that I would not scare him by talking about nuclear bombs, climate change, or today's politics.

As long as he didn't scare *me*, I insisted, by talking about smallpox, polio, or recounting what he went through in the Civil War.

A Model of Perfection

Photos of beautiful fashion models have adorned the glossy pages of magazines for decades. The stylish elegance of each artful pose underscores the natural and seemingly perpetual poise of those pictured. So ever-present is their effortless style that it would not be unexpected to see them strike an equally glamorous pose in the park while picking up dog poop. Stooping gracefully, the silky folds of their stylish fashions would drape over the soft curves of their bodies with the refinement of a fine wine being poured in slow motion into a crystal goblet.

Male models, likewise, have a place in this elite world of suave sophistication. Though not as outwardly glamorous as their female counterparts, they too, flaunt their anonymous stardom while displaying an equally natural tendency toward stylish poise. Their confident bravado shines through in their self-assured demeanor. Their nonchalant swagger reinforces the trendy fashion statements they so impeccably personify.

My brief and intermittent career as a model was not so glamorous. I did not exemplify the effortless style of those who graced the pages of *Vogue* and *Gentlemen's Quarterly*. The advertisements so many years ago that featured my likeness did not have that charismatic appeal. Women were not lingering over the images of my seductive form. It did not cause other men to secretly wish they could be more like me. Missing was the stylish poise, and the self-assured posture. And the swagger was totally nonexistent.

This lack of appeal, however, is not to be viewed as a failure. My brief modeling career capitalized on a unique quality unattainable to even the most highly-paid, successful models of the day. Yet I was able to effortlessly draw upon this distinguishing characteristic to the great benefit of the many companies and name brands in whose ads I appeared. It was an undefinable yet undeniable quality to which I was heir. And it was this special quality that kept photographers coming back for more.

Some might call it charisma. Others might see it as star quality. Actually, to my knowledge, my mother is the only one who ever used such glowing terms. To everyone else, including the photographers who hired me, it was unmistakably recognized as goofy, weird, and quirky. Or, if they were being polite, offbeat. Today it might be referred to as geeky or nerdy. My skinny frame, oversize eyeglasses, and kinky hair accentuated this unique look.

This did not, however, prevent photographers from pairing me in many cases with beautiful female models who, depending on the product being advertised, would sometimes be forced to cuddle up next to me and smile while using their best acting skills to ignore my weird idiosyncrasies. Shoe companies, banks, furniture stores, and even the YMCA recognized the advantages of departing from the norm.

The generic good looks of people who dominated magazine and newspaper ads back in the 1970s were quickly dismissed as simply more of the same boring perfection. Ads that featured such predictable images often did not cause readers to even notice the ads as the bland images were easily overlooked. Advertisers eventually became convinced that doing something out of the ordinary might have positive effects. And it was worth the risk of being different if it meant more readers would notice their ads.

Editorials, too, recognized the benefits of being unpredictable. Such was the case when *Boston Magazine* ran a feature article entitled "Models in Boston." Although the article was primarily to highlight the lives and careers of traditional fashion models, it was felt that an unconventional lead photo would attract more attention than a more predictable one.

The renowned fashion photographer who was to provide images for the article conceived an idea for an unusual lead photo that would feature some equipment, props, and other aspects involved in a typical fashion shoot. When booking me for the shoot, he had told me only that I would be working with another model and that my wardrobe would be provided at the studio. Details, however, were sketchy.

Upon arriving at his Boston studio, I walked onto the set where an array of huge lights had already been positioned. A tripod stood ready with a Nikon camera mounted on top. I did a double-take, however, when I noticed that the camera was pointed at a seamless backdrop where stood another tripod on which was mounted yet another camera. Seeing my perplexed expression, he described the shot he had conceived that would be the main image on the lead page of the article—a huge color photo that would dominate the page and lead readers into the feature article.

"It's kind of a reversal of a typical fashion shoot," he explained. "People are used to seeing the results of a fashion shoot but don't think much about the process of shooting. To call attention to the process," he continued, "we'll position a fashion model behind the camera instead of in front of it. She'll assume the opposite role she would normally take and mimic the role of the photographer by pretending to take a photo of another model. You'll be that other model."

"Okay I get it," I replied slowly with a puzzled look. "A model taking a photo of another model. Great. As long as I get paid."

With that, he directed me over to the wardrobe stylist who sat off to one side in front of a large suitcase. As I approached, she handed me a pair of flimsy men's bikini underwear. I stood with an amused expression on my face waiting for the remainder of my wardrobe.

"That's it," she said with a smirk.

I politely laughed, not wanting to be left out of the joke, but stood patiently in front of her as she turned to rummage through a suitcase of other items. Seeing that I had not moved, she closed the suitcase and looked up at me.

"Go put it on," she said abruptly.

This time there was no hint of amusement. No funny smirk. I looked down for a closer look at the skimpy undergarment I held in my hand and noticed a colorful image of the cartoon character, Tweety Bird, on the front. Just as I was about to grudgingly head to the dressing room, she turned again to her suitcase.

"Oh wait! I almost forgot," she said. "This is for you too."

"*Whew,*" I thought to myself with some relief. "*She almost had me there.*"

The stylist turned back to me and handed me a small Teddy bear.

"Okay, you're all set now."

This time she did not wait for my amused reaction. She abruptly stood and walked over to a young woman who had just entered the studio and whom I assumed to be the fashion model I would be working with. As the stylist led the young woman over to another suitcase, I slowly headed for the dressing room with my meager wardrobe.

Several minutes later, I reluctantly emerged slightly embarrassed onto a brightly-lit set with the photographer, two assistants, and the stylist all awaiting my appearance. The photographer beamed gleefully as he showed me to my mark and positioned me according to his plan. He explained the expressions and gestures he would be directing me to follow once we got started, adding that I was uniquely qualified to make this shot work.

I nonchalantly held the Teddy bear directly in front of my crotch as we all waited for the appearance of the female model. I could see by her feet protruding from a gap under her dressing room door that she had been outfitted with a stylish pair of red high heels as part of her wardrobe. I secretly hoped she would not take one look at me and walk off the set, refusing to be photographed with someone who looked like the "before" photo in a men's fitness ad.

At last she emerged from her dressing room wearing her

red high heels and... actually, that was about all she was wearing. Like me, she had been outfitted with only bikini underwear. On her graceful figure, however, it did not have the ridiculously comical appearance that I so flagrantly exemplified—a fact of which I was becoming increasingly aware as I stood self-consciously in front of my glamorous modeling partner.

The photographer directed her to stand in back of the large camera that had been placed on the set as a prop. He then instructed her to place her head under the shroud on the back of the camera, effectively removing her identity from view in the photograph. I imagined her relief in realizing that her modeling career would not be trashed by being recognized in a photo with a ridiculously unfashionable male model.

"How ironic," I thought. The only face worth seeing would be the only face not seen. Readers turning to the first page of the article expecting to see images of beautiful models would instead see that of a skinny geek displaying way too much of himself.

The camera clicked and lights flashed incessantly as the photographer worked his magic. As digital cameras had not yet made their appearance, he exposed a great many rolls of Kodak film, directing me to alter my pose and facial expressions every few minutes. After what seemed an eternity, the shoot mercifully came to its conclusion, and I was able to finally get dressed. Upon emerging from the dressing room, I approached the wardrobe stylist and handed her the Tweety Bird underwear. With an expression I can only describe as that of one who has just tasted sour milk, she held up her hands and turned away.

"Uhh... you can keep those," she pleaded.

In the end, the results of that day's photography session would not make the final cut to appear in *Boston Magazine*. Upon viewing the results, the editors ultimately determined it did not reflect the clean-cut and serious image they wanted to project. Had I been a full-time, professional model, I no doubt would have been insulted by the blatant rejection. I would have taken great exception to the fact that my likeness was deemed unfit for their readers to see. The body I see in the mirror each morning was, in their opinion, not worthy of a small place on one of their precious pages.

Now, almost fifty years later, as I reflect back on that experience, it is the final selected photo from that photo shoot that brings a smile to my face. Although this photo ultimately did not make it into the publication, thousands of published copies circulating throughout the state of Massachusetts would not have enhanced the memory of that day. The one print I have retained all these years is possibly the only lasting image that remains as proof that the shoot ever happened. At the risk of once again being ridiculed, it is my pleasure to now share that photo on the following page with those of you who have taken the time to read this story. But only if you promise not to laugh.

Just kidding. Go ahead and laugh.

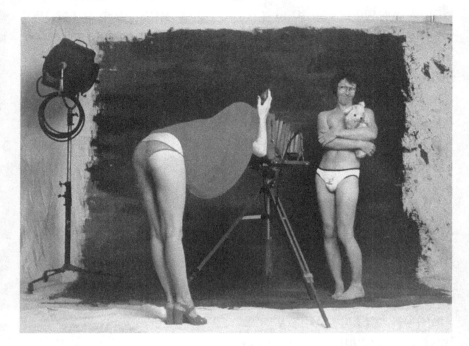

Note to Self

When the waiter asks me whether I want my Palak Paneer mild, medium, or spicy, remind me never to say spicy. I made that mistake on my first dinner date with the woman who, despite what transpired, agreed to become my wife. After she ordered her tandoori chicken spicy, I figured I'd show her I'm no wimp.

"Spicy," I confidently told the waiter.

Big mistake. The first bite was fine. Second bite, okay. By the fifth or sixth fork full, however, beads of sweat were beginning to form on my forehead and she noticed I was turning red.

"Are you okay," she asked quietly, but with some alarm.

"Yeah, I'm... hagh... haaa. I'm fine."

I could feel myself becoming progressively more in distress and half expected the smoke detectors to go off at any moment. By the time the meal had mercifully come to an end, I had made a promise to myself to admit that my delicate palette is no match for the habanero chili peppers and other sadistic spices that are liberally simmered into every molecule of many ethnic dishes. I have come to embrace my status as a spice wimp. Now, whenever we go out and share a meal of Indian, Mexican, or Thai food and the waiter asks if we want mild, medium, or spicy, we always compromise. We ask for mild.

And while we're on the subject of food, remind me to stay away from mail-order sushi. Not that the opportunity has ever presented itself, but based on the questionable food decisions I've made over the years, I figure it's only a matter of time before such a far-fetched offering is presented.

By the way, I need to remember that those cute little icons of fire next to some items on the menu do not mean those selections have been delicately roasted over an open flame. It means my mouth will be engulfed in flames after the second bite.

Remembering to do or not to do certain things is sometimes difficult. Things we do without even thinking are the very things that usually get us into trouble.

I have to keep reminding myself whenever I'm texting a friend that "LOL" means "laugh out loud," not "lots of love." Sending someone a message that says, for example, "Sorry your dog died. LOL" would be a very inconsiderate thing to do. Sorry Nancy.

And speaking of laughing, remind me not to laugh when my friend steps in dog poop. That's the best way of ensuring that my turn is next. And believe me, the follow-up laugh is always louder than the first one.

And remind me not to put my wife's stretch tights in the dryer. Oh they come out dry alright, but they look like they were made for a four-year-old little girl... Every time. I'd get into less trouble if I pretended not to know where the dryer is.

Everyday things around the house have always been a good way for me to show that I'm not paying attention. If I'd thought about it, I would have known that hanging the fly swatter in the closet next to my wife's brand new sweater was not a good idea. Remind me never to do that again. I know it sounds pretty basic, but trust me, paying attention is not as easy as it looks on other people. Common sense isn't always that common.

Case in point: I once wore my Boston Red Sox cap on a trip to New York City. Remind me never to do that again. No matter where the two teams are in the standings, you're going to hear about it either way. I like New York. But New Yorkers can be very loud in expressing their opinions. If the Sox are up on the Yankees, you'll hear a chorus of "boooos" from people as they walk past you on the street. If, on the other hand, the Yankees are up on the Sox, you'll be ridiculed for being a loser.

And there's something I need to remember whenever I hear that TV commercial about putting your investments on a new path. I need to be reminded that what they're saying is "new direction" not "nude erection." Actually, I don't need to be reminded. Two seconds after I hear it I slap myself on the forehead and roll my eyes. It would be nice, however, if I could remember at the beginning of the commercial to prepare myself for what's to come. Being caught off-guard every time is getting ridiculous.

And remind me to always check the rearview mirror in my car before I back up. Not that I've ever run over a puppy or some stray child, but after seeing my neighbor run over his inflatable air mattress, I wouldn't want anyone to laugh at me as much as I laughed at him. Although I must say, the sound it made was hilarious.

And while we're on the subject of cars, remind me never to ride in the back seat of a convertible when someone riding in the front seat is licking an ice cream cone. I was only twelve at the time, so I can't be faulted too much for not knowing any better. And it was my first ride in a car with the top down, so I was excited at the prospect of shouting into the headwind and having other people wish they were me. My Boy Scout leader had treated a few of us with a trip to the local dairy bar. But even more of a thrill was the sixty-mile-an-hour joyride in his little sports car that followed. I was crammed into the back along with my friend, Richard, where there was actually no rear seat, but only a narrow space for luggage. It didn't matter, though. The thrill of speeding past families cooped up in their slow-moving sedans was enough of an adventure. The exhilaration of feeling the wind whip through our hair and... what's this? Is that ice cream splattering all over my face and eyeglasses with sixty-mile-per-hour droplets?

By the time we got back to the town hall, the entire front of my uniform was soaked with sticky, vanilla ice cream. Vanilla! It wasn't even a good flavor. And while I might not have been at fault, you'd think my scoutmaster would have known what a mess would result from such high-speed revelry. Or, perhaps it was his cunning way of protecting the back of his shiny convertible by strategically placing two unsuspecting kids to absorb all the incoming flak. At any rate, the next time someone invites me out for ice cream in their convertible, remind me to ask if I can drive.

As you can see, there are so many things I need to constantly remind myself of. Like never to eat a family size bag of potato chips by myself, even if my close friends tell me I'm like family to them. And when visiting another city, to never ask my cab driver to take me to his favorite casual restaurant. Not only did I forget to mention that I'm a vegetarian, but Chuck E. Cheese isn't all it's cracked up to be.

And I always need to remind myself to pull back the shower curtain to see if there's a serial killer hiding there. As of this writing, I've not discovered one yet, but one can't be too careful. It's not always that easy to remember all of this. And although my lapse of memory sometimes lasts for no more than a second or two, a second or two is all it takes to ruin my day. And my new shirt. So remind me to always close the sun roof *before* driving through the car wash.

Whether I'm reminding myself to *never* do something or to *always* do something there's another very important thing I need to remember. There are no absolute rules when it comes to behavior. Circumstances change. What makes sense at any given time may not make sense at another time. Although rules of common sense hold true in most situations, there may inevitably be exceptions. So in light of this possibility, the most important rule I need to remind myself of is that "always" and "never" are two words I should always remember never to use.

Shakespeare Got it Wrong

It was Shakespeare who wrote, *"What's in a name? A Rose by any other name would smell as sweet."*

I can't say that I had Shakespeare in mind when I named my cat "Mister Brown." I was just trying to be funny. I was also trying to show that the name or label we give to something does not matter. The name does not define it. It does not change its inherent characteristics. You see, not only was Mister Brown a female, but she was white.

Actually, having just committed that assertion to print, I'm now already having second thoughts. I'm beginning to think that sometimes a name may indeed have the power to define something and change how we see it.

Shakespeare too, may have been misinformed. If what we call a rose had instead been called a bloody stool sample, I doubt if we'd still be buying bouquets of them on Valentines Day to give to our sweethearts. "Honey, I just bought you a whole bunch of bloody stool samples. Would you like to smell them?"

Likewise, if Walt Disney had named his cute little rodent cartoon character Ricky Rat instead of Mickey Mouse, his character probably would have looked no different, though I doubt if kids would still think he was so cute.

When Johnny Cash recorded the ballad "A Boy Named Sue," he sang about the profound impact the misnomer had made in the life of one so inappropriately named. You see, by the end of the song, Sue had come to realize that being so named actually had a positive effect. Although, according to Cash, *"life ain't easy for a boy named Sue,"* he had become tougher and able to overcome adversity as a result. According to the lyrics, when the boy's father left his mother knowing he wouldn't be around to help raise his son, he intentionally gave him the name Sue to toughen him up in order to help him survive the cruel world without a dad. Ultimately, Sue had come to learn by necessity to stand up to bullies and ridicule.

Okay, I doubt if there ever existed an actual boy named Sue. Despite the positive lesson the boy in the song supposedly learned as a result, however, the negative effects of such a name would have far outweighed any positive effects and plagued a boy named Sue for eternity. Such an inappropriate name would almost certainly have residual and lasting adverse consequences. Why do you think you never see cute little newborn babies named Adolf?

Knowing that something as simple as a name can affect how people see it, it is difficult to understand how some names come to exist. I'll never understand the thought process of the cosmetics genius who named his lightly-scented perfume "toilet water." Did he think the allure of such a name would have women everywhere rushing out to buy it and apply it to their skin? Did he think this was the secret potion that would have them saying, "Finally, the smell no man can resist." Did he think by naming his product toilet water he'd have men everywhere saying, "Wow! She really knows what turns me on." He obviously did not listen to his wife when she said, "What the F--- are you thinking?"

The same logic would apply in reverse. Names or labels have been assigned to things to give people a positive perception. If given a choice, few people would order "calves brains" or "lamb glands" from a restaurant menu. However, when chefs refer to them by their more appetizing name, "sweetbreads," they sound more like a culinary delicacy. Even I might be tempted to order them. And I'm a vegetarian!

The fallacy of Shakespeare's assertion that names do not matter is also well understood by sports teams. Consider the Golden State Warriors, Atlanta Braves, Los Angeles Chargers, and the host of other teams so named to conjure up images of fierce fighters. The fear and dread induced by the likes of the Lions, Tigers, Pirates, and Giants would be considerably diminished were their rivals to suddenly find themselves taking the field against the Detroit Teddy Bears or the Pittsburgh Pansies.

This phenomenon is not, by any means, new. Over one thousand years ago, a Norseman by the name of Eric the Red was exiled to a frozen and icy island in the North Atlantic. Knowing the power a name has in determining one's perception, he named the snowy wilderness Greenland in hopes of misleading people and getting more of them to settle there. In an ironic contrast, Iceland, the island from which he was banished, has a much milder climate due to the warm Atlantic current and, as a result, is mostly green. On a recent visit to Iceland's capital city, Reykjavik, a shopkeeper informed me that, in fact, it hardly ever snows there.

Shakespeare may have misinformed us by insisting that a name has no effect on something. But he did it with such literary flair and elegance that if I am ever lucky enough to meet him, I'll not make him feel bad by telling him he was mistaken.

The Bravest Man in the World

As the sun retreated from a cloudless sky on a mild September evening, I dined with close friends outside at one of our favorite local seafood restaurants. We were only a mile or so from the beautiful seacoast of New England, and the bounty we were about to enjoy had arrived here from local fishing grounds. We watched with eager anticipation as the waitress delivered a huge tray of oysters on the half-shell and carefully placed it down in front of us.

We raised our glasses of chilled Chardonnay and brought them slowly together with a gentle clink. As the others voiced salutes of "cheers," I closed my eyes and silently paid tribute to those brave men whose extreme courage had made this moment possible. If not for them, we doubtless would not be about to enjoy this delectable repast in such a peaceful setting, free of all cares and worries. As a warm breeze washed over us, I was grateful for the dauntless courage of those fearless men who, in past generations, had displayed their valor in making all this possible. They had thrown caution to the wind and faced down adversity in their selfless sacrifice in order that future generations might partake of what this great land has to offer. Their unprecedented bravery was about to be consummated as we shared this simple, but elegant meal.

I studied the three dozen oysters artfully arranged before us—smears of congealed, beige phlegm sitting in limpid puddles of brackish liquid and cradled in rock-hard, crusty pieces of seashell. I picked up one specimen and as I held it up to my face preparing to let it slide into my mouth, my overwhelming gratitude once again rose to the forefront of my mind. I thought about those intrepid individuals whose heroism was about to be made manifest in this shared feast in a land of plenty. I thought about how they had come face to face with the unknown in a dangerous world. I thought about the many hardships they had overcome to make our beautiful evening of dining out a reality.

There have been generations of countless soldiers marching into battle clutching their weapons and facing the threat of a deadly enemy. The outcome, though uncertain, was sure to be a horrific death for many of the combatants on both sides. But that's not who I'm talking about. I'm talking about the bravery of those anonymous, yet courageous forebearers who settled on the shores of this strange and foreign land and whose heroism improved the lives of future generations. I'm talking about that brave individual who was the very first one to ever eat a raw oyster.

No doubt, he had scoured the seashore for hours looking for any morsel to eat, and was so deprived of sustenance at that point, that he would have eaten practically anything. Even a slimy bivalve mollusk he found lying dead in a pool of brackish salt water with all its innards intact, including its digestive tract, gills, rectum, anus, and glands of all sorts.

Actually, that's exactly what he did. So don't tell me he wasn't the bravest man in the world.

We now consider them a delicacy and look forward to them appearing on restaurant menus as oyster season rolls around each year. We happily pay a premium price for the privilege of carefully spooning on a little horseradish and cocktail sauce as we slurp up the squishy creatures by the dozen. And as they slide down, our only thought is how delicious they taste. No thought is given to the primitive life form lying in the mucky sand among the decaying seaweed and encased in a dirty and smelly shell. There is no acknowledgment of the fact that the creature has not been cooked or otherwise prepared in any way to resemble what normally would pass as food, but harvested entirely as it was found and simply left to die in its shell.

This, however, is quite possibly what was on the mind of that very first person who dredged up the unlikely specimen from the swampy residue of low tide. After smashing open the gritty shell and studying the shapeless, visceral mass at close range, he said to himself, "Mmmm, that looks delicious."

Okay, that's probably not what he said. He no doubt held his nose at the putrid sight, closed his eyes as he slurped the dead slime into his mouth and said, "Well, I either eat this, or I die of starvation." He had no idea if eating such an unlikely mass of gel that he found lying in the sand might actually be his cause of death. But he tempted fate, opened his mouth and swallowed.

We owe a debt of gratitude to that anonymous trailblazer who, at some time in the far-distant past, paved the unlikely way to a culinary delight. His bravery does not go unnoticed as I bring another oyster to my mouth and once again raise my glass in tribute.

"This one's for you. Cheers!"

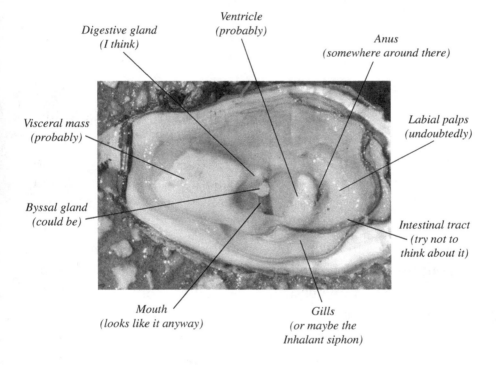

Digestive gland
(I think)

Ventricle
(probably)

Anus
(somewhere around there)

Visceral mass
(probably)

Labial palps
(undoubtedly)

Byssal gland
(could be)

Intestinal tract
(try not to
think about it)

Mouth
(looks like it anyway)

Gills
(or maybe the
Inhalant siphon)

Truth Be Told

The burly, tattooed guy stood in front of me in line with his girlfriend as we both waited for tables at a local restaurant. Out of the corner of my eye I could see a skull with horns emblazoned on the side of his neck, and what looked like an eagle grasping something in its talons. Elaborate spider webs covered nearly all of his upper arms making it difficult for me to read the words also inscribed there. Glancing down, I noticed a New England Patriots logo on the side of one calf. When he caught me casually perusing his collection of symbols he stared back at me as if waiting for me to comment.

Not to disappoint, I acknowledged the embarrassing standoff by first saying hello. I then filled the long silence by noting the long wait to be seated. He nodded in response, still awaiting my comment on the tapestry of ink work of which he was obviously very proud.

"Is that a New England Patriots team logo on your calf?" I finally asked.

Turning to afford me a better look, he noted that it indeed was one of his more recent additions.

"Well, I'm the attorney for the New England Patriots,"

I began. "Are you aware that's a violation of copyright law?"

No response.

"To date, we've prosecuted sixteen such infringements of our brand," I added.

The confrontation continued for only a few seconds before I softened my expression in an effort to ease his discomfort. (And to avoid my being punched in the face.) I told him I was just trying to be funny. That I wasn't really a lawyer. And that I don't even watch football. The standoff mercifully ended when the hostess approached and announced, "table for two."

It would not be the first time I pretended to be someone I'm not. My cousin, Leta, was visiting from the west coast and I was seeing her five-year-old daughter for the first time since infancy. We were all at the dining room table when Leta turned to her young daughter and said, "David has a very interesting job. You should ask him what he does."

With some skepticism, the child bashfully looked at me and asked, "What do you do?"

Without hesitation, but with all the nonchalance I could muster, I replied, "I'm an astronaut."

A blank stare signaled her disinterest and there were no followup questions.

"I'm just kidding," I finally laughed. "I'm an artist."

Her blank stare was quickly overridden by wide eyes and a big smile. She immediately added with much excitement, "Will you draw a picture for me?"

Sometimes the truth of who you are can actually be more interesting than what you pretend to be. But pretending still holds a certain fascination. Sometimes it comes about not because of what you say, but because of what you don't say. Left to their own devices, people may make their own mistaken assumptions which, if left uncorrected, allow you to assume a counterfeit identity by default.

I approached two people in the parking lot as they hovered around a huge motorcycle dripping with chrome. The couple appeared to be in their early twenties and as I got closer, I realized that the young man had his camera in hand and his girlfriend was posing for a photo next to the big machine. I continued to walk directly toward them, but when they noticed me approaching, they quickly stepped away from the motorcycle. I was a mere six feet from them when the girl sheepishly apologized assuring me that they weren't touching the motorcycle, and that they hoped I didn't mind them getting so close.

Her boyfriend then added in a friendly tone, "It's a great looking bike and we just wanted a few photos. I hope you don't mind. We didn't touch it."

It was then I realized that they thought the bike belonged to me.

"Yeah, she's a beauty isn't she," I offered, pretending to actually know about something I've never even ridden on. "Harley Davidsons have always been my favorite."

Feeling the tension dissipate, the girl asked if I'd mind if she sat on the bike for one last photo. Doing nothing to dissuade her from the mistaken belief that the bike was mine, I let her know that I had no objection. She immediately climbed up and sat astride the huge seat as she leaned into the wide handlebars as her boyfriend started clicking away.

After the photo-opp had run its course, they were totally

stunned when I climbed into the car next to the big bike and drove away. I could see them in my rear view mirror hurrying to distance themselves from the scene.

Then there was the time I rushed back to the office from lunch because I remembered I had an appointment with a woman who was interviewing for a job as a graphic designer. I burst through the door into the reception room, and saw a young lady sitting patiently with her portfolio at her side. I looked at my watch and plopped myself down in a chair beside her in the waiting room.

We sat in silence watching the clock on the wall tick off the minutes. Finally she turned to me and asked, "Are you here for an interview too?"

I was not lying when I answered, "As a matter of fact, I am."

Another minute passed and I asked her what job she was applying for.

"Graphic designer," she proudly said. "It's a freelance position. I'm here to see David Random. I hear he's a good person to work for."

I was also not lying when I agreed with her and responded, "Yes, I've heard that too. From many many people in the business. He's definitely one of the best. And such a talented person as well. He's great!"

Okay, maybe I overdid it a little. I then asked her if I could take a look at her portfolio while we waited, and she, without hesitation picked it up and opened it for me to see. She led me through each page of her work as I asked the appropriate questions about how long she'd been doing this type of work, who she had worked for in the past, and so on.

We landed on the final page of her portfolio and she turned to me again and said, "By the way, my name's Abby."

I reached out to shake her hand and said, "And I'm David... David Random."

As her jaw dropped open, I added, "And you got the job."

I confess to occasionally having stretched the truth or misleading people by omission. Sometimes to be funny. Sometimes to make a point. Truth be told, it's sometimes just to see what I can get away with. Sometimes when you make up stories it's easy to make people believe them. Often, people believe something simply because they want to believe it. Case in point, of the four stories I just related to you, one of them was a complete fabrication. See how easy that was?

Taking Dining to New Heights

The business meeting lasted longer than expected so we now had to hurry. We raced down the elevator and out onto West 23rd Street to hail a taxi. The four of us piled in and gave the cabbie the address of the restaurant to which we had just called in an order of Chinese take-out food. Since the company was paying, we had spared no expense, loading up on Shrimp Lo Mein, Szechuan Spicy Chicken, Egg Foo Yong, and an astoundingly large array of appetizers. After hurriedly picking up our dinner, we once again crammed into the cab and headed out of New York City with enough food to last several days, hoping to catch the next flight from La Guardia to Boston.

We made the seven o'clock flight with only minutes to spare as we rushed aboard and shuffled our way down the aisle, our arms loaded down under the weight of our Chinese feast. By the time we found seats, heads were turning in our direction from all over the plane, as the smell of our dinner followed us all the way from the cockpit to row thirty-five. Although the plane was filled to less than capacity, we ended up way back in the smoking section because it was the only place where we could find four seats together. In those days, smoking was allowed on most commercial flights, although smokers were restricted to a certain section of the plane, usually toward the back. No matter, our dinner awaited and it was all we could think about. After a full day of meetings, we had managed only a quick lunch of a bagel and cream cheese. We would now make up for it, even if it meant inhaling the second-hand exhaust from Marlboros and Camels.

The plane took forever to taxi out to the runway and take off, but once airborne, we reached cruising altitude quickly. When the flight attendant finally announced that we were allowed to open our tray tables, we did so before she even finished her announcement, as one bag after another was opened and spread out in front of us. When our smorgasbord was fully unveiled, it covered not only our own tray tables, but those of two empty seats in our vicinity. More heads started turning toward the back of the plane to sniff the unexpectedly aromatic air, and an unusually large number of passengers began taking "curiosity strolls" down the aisle to see what the flight attendant was cooking back in the galley kitchen. When passengers saw the full extent of our buffet, most acknowledged our spread with big smiles that seemed to say "Why didn't I think of that?" Even the stewardess seemed impressed, though she declined our gracious offer to grab a plate and help herself.

It was a more innocent world back in the 1970s, and airports reflected the relaxed attitudes with less constrained regulations. TSA screening was fairly lax as you headed through check-in. No one looked to see if you were hiding a bomb in your shoe. Everything was so casual and laid back that when we were asked what was in our bags, it was less about "Are you carrying guns and ammunition" than it was about "Mmm, smells good. Can I have a taste?" They were more concerned that you didn't spill chow mein on the seat.

We were frequent flyers on Eastern Airlines, which touted itself as "the second largest airline in the free world," and we regularly migrated from Boston to New York and back on the Eastern Shuttle, taking advantage of its every-hour-on-the-hour flights. It was a nonchalant affair with little pre-planning. There were no reservations, no tickets, and no assigned seats. You simply boarded when you wanted and sat wherever you liked. Often, there was no jetway and passengers just walked out across the tarmac and climbed the stairs directly into the plane. If it was raining, you were handed an umbrella. Once airborne, the flight attendant came down the aisle and you paid the sixteen-dollar airfare with a credit card while already halfway to your destination.

In the 1980s however, a crippling labor dispute led to the airline's downfall, and under former astronaut Frank Borman's leadership, Eastern was eventually forced to liquidate. It was the end of an era of casual and effortless jet travel. And it was the beginning of a more suspicious world.

As time passed, terrorist activities became more commonplace prompting regulations to be updated accordingly. Our portable Chinese feast would have been unthinkable during this new era of widespread suspicion. Commercial airline passengers were subjected to an obstacle course of searches that, at times, seemed to go overboard. Passengers were now required to remove their belts and totally empty their pockets. They were required to remove their shoes which led to a renewed popularity of slip-on loafers, and the regrettable invention of Crocs.

Travelers suddenly found themselves having to purge items normally carried on board with little thought. If you tried to pass through the gate with a bottle of shampoo that was larger than three ounces, you had to either throw it out or use it all up on the spot. I once had a pair of nail clippers confiscated because an overzealous TSA agent thought it quite possible that I might burst unannounced into the cockpit to give the unsuspecting pilot a manicure. I thought it strange that such a tiny innocent item would be confiscated, yet I was allowed to carry my car keys on board which, as far as anyone knew, could have been honed to a razor-sharp edge and used to slit someone's throat.

As regulations regarding boarding procedures became more strict, however, my colleagues and I accepted it as a challenge to play practical jokes on fellow employees. One workmate in particular became the brunt of our depraved activity due to the fact that she displayed more embarrassment than did our other fellow employees. Donna perpetuated these gags by her own overreactions. Had she failed to show such humiliation, we would have stopped immediately and found subjects more easily embarrassed at discovering surprising and questionable items in their carry-ons. She was, however, the perfect target because of the enormous, full length fur coat she wore all winter, making the items we stuffed into the bulky pockets undetectable even to her until she was face to face with TSA agents. No one was more surprised than Donna to pull small cucumbers, dog biscuits, pine cones, and a host of other inappropriate and embarrassing items from the hidden recesses of her deep pockets.

Occasionally, items would not be discovered until an unusual image showed up on the scanning machine. Only then would the full extent of Donna's carry-on items be revealed to the gate agent and curious fellow passengers within close proximity.

My favorite prank was the day she unloaded her pockets only to find a single raw hot dog in a clear plastic baggie. The TSA folks are probably still talking about that crazy lady carrying raw meat. We were always careful, however, not to stash anything that would make Donna look dangerous. It was rewarding enough to simply make her look stupid.

Peter was another frequent target of our undercover activities. Peter packed light and didn't usually carry much more than his briefcase on his regular day-trips to the New York office. That, however, provided quite enough opportunity to hide little surprises for him. Inside his briefcase he usually carried a book to read while on the flight, so that became the spot where we'd hide his surprises. Tucked innocuously between the pages of his book we'd place various shapes cut from sheets of aluminum foil, undetectable to Peter as he showed up at the TSA checkpoint. Nothing seemed out of the ordinary until his bag went through the scanner. Then with all the subtlety of a locomotive passing through your living room, strange shapes popped up on the screen.

We were always careful not to cut out any shape that would get Peter (or us) into trouble—No guns, no daggers. But cutouts of a penis were fair game.

Eventually, the pranks finally came to an end. I'm not sure whether we just grew tired of playing the same tricks on the same people or if it had something to do with the fact that the ad agency we worked for landed a commercial airline as an account. As we started to do the airline's advertising, we began to realize the seriousness of screening travelers before they boarded their flights. None of us wanted to be the one responsible for jeopardizing an account by unwittingly forcing the airport gate agents to take part in our tasteless jokes.

Having become accustomed to the new rules of flying, I now see today's strict regulations as just a minor inconvenience, and a small price to pay for the safety and reassurance of air travelers. I check in wearing my slip-on shoes, and I leave my nail clippers at home. I do occasionally think, however, as I'm rationed a tiny bag of peanuts by the flight attendant, "Boy, I could really go for some Chinese food."

A Bedtime Story

My wife has a snoring problem... Me.

She has made repeated accusations that in the dead of night, abrupt, guttural sounds emanate from my open mouth. And although she is not prone to fabrication or even exaggeration, I cannot corroborate her assertion. Since I am peacefully asleep during the purported offenses, I have never heard a sound. Nor have I ever awakened myself with such disturbances to which she claims to bear witness. She once tried to record the occurrence by setting a portable tape recorder on her nightstand in hopes of capturing the event, and quelling my denials. The next morning, she claimed that the lack of any sound captured on the tape was due to a recorder malfunction.

I, therefore, feel an obligation to advise the reader that the words I write here, while I have every reason to believe their truthfulness, are in fact based on hearsay. Aside from the wandering moans of our new cat, Maui, who is still learning his new surroundings, the only interruptions I am ever aware of at night are the prods from my sleep partner. These come, she says, in immediate retaliation for my snoring. I politely roll onto my other side to resume an otherwise restful sleep.

On occasion it has driven her to seek refuge in a part of the house sufficiently distant to allow the resumption of her own well-deserved rest.

I have tried the throat sprays, the nose sprays, the pills, the drops. She has tried earplugs. I even went for several sessions to a doctor who, with the aid of a laptop computer hooked up to my wrists, ankles and forehead, directed waves of energy to the affected areas. As far-fetched as this sounds, it did have some interesting results, but I'll save that for another story.

It is this sequence of events that finds me here at a snore clinic west of Boston, just across the street from the world-famous Lahey Clinic. I mention the latter only to lend some degree of credibility to what you might otherwise picture in a strip mall next to a Dunkin Donuts. The office, though small, looks very professional, and I am encouraged to see that several people are actually wearing white lab coats. I've already been for my initial consultation where I filled out medical history forms. My wife, who accompanied me, filled out one section as testimony to my alleged snoring. We also watched a video in which several people claim to have been snorers and now claim it is no longer a problem. It is unclear from the video whether they were cured, or whether their spouses just moved out.

I put my skepticism aside and decide to set up an appointment to have the procedure done. "Somnoplasty" by name, is an outpatient operation in which probes are inserted into the soft tissue palette at the back of the throat and into the uvula, that little punching bag thing that hangs back there. This, of course, after several needles of a Novocaine-like substance has numbed my throat. The probes are then heated to a temperature high enough to shrink the surrounding tissue, thus opening the air passages and eliminating the vibrations that cause snoring. Had they spared me the details I would have been happier. The fact that I would now be able to visualize the hard-hat construction zone taking place in the back of my throat would have little or no bearing on its successful outcome.

Immediately following the treatment, my discomfort is minimal. As directed, I suck down a couple popsicles before leaving the office to drive myself home. Swallowing is difficult, and it is hard to talk much. Not that there is any pain. My numbed mouth just couldn't get words to come out right. Upon arriving home, I use my voice sparingly as I make an attempt to relate my recent experience to its expectant beneficiary. I talk in short sentences, and do a lot of nodding.

"How did it go?" she asks.

"Mmmmm," I nod.

"Does your throat hurt?"

"Mm-mm."

That night after a couple more popsicles, I prepare a chair in the living room to sleep, as instructed, sitting up at a 45-degree angle. This, they cautioned, is to prevent me from choking on my uvula, which has now swelled to the size of a circus balloon. I check it out in the mirror to make certain there's still room for food to pass, and I am encouraged to discover that it feels much worse than it looks. My uvula is only the size of my thumb. It is, however, dragging on my tongue, and I keep trying to swallow it.

Upon returning to the living room, my wife asks, "How

does it look?" I can only silently mouth the word, "Wow!"

The following morning shows little change in my discomfort, but by the end of the second day, I am noticing definite signs of normal speech. I'm also dying to clear my throat, but that's forbidden until day four. The doctor says after a week of no soup, hot drinks, or spicy food, my throat will start to feel normal.

From then on, it's a waiting game as the treatment takes its full effect. The post-treatment instruction sheet says that in about four to eight weeks I should be well on my way to sleeping through the night in peaceful silence.

Oh wait... I already do that.

Becoming Prey

No sooner had I stepped from the car when the attack began. In an instant I was surrounded by the grayish-brown creatures biting at me from all sides, their huge green eyes darting back and forth like crazed demons. Fending off an attacker on one side left the opposite flank unprotected and vulnerable to more vicious attacks that seemed to come out of nowhere with lightning speed. The assault was unrelenting and I dashed the final fifty feet to the safety of the house, stumbling over the loose gravel of the driveway in a futile attempt to outrun the attackers.

It was not until I had slammed the front door firmly behind me that I was able to close my eyes and force a deliberate breath from my mouth with audible relief. Had an item fallen from my bag of groceries on my mad dash for safety, it is questionable whether I would have gone back to retrieve it. Very little could have persuaded me to go back and face certain attack by the bloodthirsty predators waiting only a few feet away on the other side of the door and ready to take full advantage of such a momentary lapse of good judgment.

In this part of the country they torment and intimidate

local residents, holding entire communities under siege for weeks at a time, making even the most hardy individuals afraid to leave their homes and venture outside. This would not be the first time I had been attacked by these predators, and I knew that their savage bites were vicious and painful.

It was not a pack of snarling wolves, nor carnivorous wild dogs that caused such trepidation, though they were certainly ferocious enough. Nor was it their appearance or size that was so intimidating. In fact, they were no larger that my thumbnail. It was their unrelenting onslaught in such staggering numbers and the acute pain they could inflict that kept people prisoners in their own homes for a few weeks each July.

Try to explain "greenheads" to someone from another part of the country and they would snort incredulously at what must certainly be an exaggeration. Mention the flying, carnivorous insects to anyone living near the salt water marshes of the northeast, however, and their reaction would be quite different. To the human species that has become prey, greenheads are a serious consideration for any activity that involves being outdoors. Even going to the mailbox is often postponed until after dark when the threat of being attacked is less likely.

On certain days each summer, a sign posted at the Crane's Beach parking lot in Ipswich, Massachusetts warns, "Greenheads are biting today. No refunds." This terse warning is mainly for the benefit of non-residents unfamiliar with the plague of the insufferable insects and who, in moments of ill-advised disregard, shrug their shoulders and rationalize, "I don't mind a few little nips. How bad could it be? Besides, I have insect repellent." The great majority of those who do not heed this warning are chased back to their cars, flailing wildly after only a few unbearable minutes, where they happily forego the parking fee in exchange for the safety of their vehicles.

Tabanus nigrovittatus, as they are respectfully known to those who study the species, are highly resistant to all types of repellents, and are virtually indestructible. Their mouth parts are designed not for piercing, but for tearing. And unlike slow-moving mosquitoes whose relatively dainty bite is preceded by a feeble buzzing sound alerting you to their presence, and giving you ample time to take aim with a carefully placed slap, greenheads give no such warning. They have also mastered the tactic of teamwork. One, or sometimes two or more, distract your attention to an unprotected patch of bare skin. While you wildly smack your ankles, three more have already attacked your neck. The first hint you have of their presence is the sharp and immediate pain that accompanies the tearing of your flesh. Even if you are quick enough to land a direct slap at the source of the pain, greenheads are capable of vacating the spot before your open hand arrives. Even when you manage a direct hit, the sturdy pests often fly off unperturbed to attempt another ambush.

Perhaps the one redeeming feature of a greenhead bite is that there are no long-lasting effects. Unlike mosquito bites, there is no swelling or lingering itch. Once the excruciating pain of having your skin ripped open is gone, it's over. That is, until the next one attacks. And there is always a next one.

My brother and I used to make a sport of swatting the greenheads that amassed in large numbers under the awnings of a tent in my parents' backyard. The concentrated groupings of flying marauders provided easy targets, though a forceful and direct hit was necessary to score points. The idea was to count how many greenheads you could kill with a single whack of a fly swatter. So dense were the clusters, that it was not uncommon to kill four or five at once.

As familiar as these pests have become to seacoast residents, the greenhead menace is a local phenomenon indeed, as one need travel only a mile or so from the marshes to escape the ravenous hordes.

On Plum Island, the eleven-mile-long barrier island off the north shore of Massachusetts, we once made the mistake of leaving our car windows cracked open to mitigate the effects of the ninety-degree day while, against our better judgment, we braved the sandy dunes. Upon our hasty return we discovered that the oven-like environment of our car was very much to the liking of the swarms of greenheads that had found the narrow openings with apparently little trouble and waited inside for an easy meal and a ride home.

It is their attraction to heated enclosures, however, that would prove to be their weakness. Beginning in the 1970s, large, black boxes started appearing on the vast salt water marshes. The oven-sized traps held above the marsh grass on wooden stilts became death chambers for the greenheads that were fatally attracted to their hot, dark interiors. And attracted they were. It is difficult to convey to a non-resident the staggering numbers in which these insects are present, but researchers from Rutgers University have reported catching as many as one thousand per hour in the black traps that dot the otherwise unspoiled landscape of the marshes. Despite the prodigious numbers that are removed from the traps by the shovelful, in practical terms, the program made barely a dent in the annual greenhead population.

While I begrudge no creature on the planet the right to exist, it is difficult to imagine a single redeeming characteristic of the lowly greenhead. What possible benefit could be derived from such an irritating pest except, perhaps, as a convenient, crispy snack for birds?

It would be difficult to imagine that anything could possibly lessen the contempt we humans feel for our flying nemesis. But for one day in 1977, that is exactly what happened. In the summer of that year,

Rows of greenhead traps dot an otherwise unspoiled salt marsh.

my family and I conceived a way for people to relate to greenheads without complaining about them. A way, in fact, to celebrate their annual invasion as an amusing diversion.

Each July in the seacoast city of Newburyport, Massachusetts, the week-long celebration known as Yankee Homecoming draws both residents and tourists with sidewalk sales, parades, concerts, fireworks, art exhibits, and road races. In addition to bringing merchants and restaurant proprietors out onto the sidewalks to sell their wares, private citizens are also allowed to set up vendor booths in the center of town. Ambitious artists and crafters spread the results of their various projects before throngs of curious pedestrians. It was during this highly anticipated, annual festival that "The Official Greenhead Swat Team" made its debut appearance. It was our tongue-in-cheek tribute to those small, ferocious spoilers of summer,

those pests of picnics, ravenous ruiners of recreation that became our celebrated, local mascots. For a few brief hours that summer, they became our swallows of Capistrano.

The Official Greenhead Swat Team existed in name only. There was nothing official about us. There were no headquarters, no mission statement, no organization, no hopes of a continued presence. The end of Yankee Homecoming week would, in fact, mark the end of its brief existence. There was absolutely no reason for its presence other than to encourage a few smiles among strangers and to sell the small, inexpensive items we had created for the sole purpose of poking fun at a mutual misery.

The center of town that day was packed with tourists and townsfolk. And although it was the height of greenhead season, people were a safe distance from the salt water marshes beyond which the greenheads did not venture. Those who wandered throughout the bustling streets and alleys were free to enjoy the day without fear of becoming easy prey. Small groups of pedestrians clustered around street musicians, jugglers, and magicians before being lured away by louder or more colorful displays. Red, white and blue banners hung from picturesque old buildings making the narrow streets look like patriotic postcards. Merchandise spilled from every shop out onto the sidewalks where tables and racks featured clothing, jewelry, souvenirs and other trinkets.

Interspersed among these shopkeepers, the other merchants-for-a-day displayed paintings, photography, quilts, and other homemade crafts. The items we had brought with us to sell at our greenhead booth were inexpensive, impulse items, all of them green in color. Embroidered patches, refrigerator magnets crafted from the heads of old wooden clothespins in the shape of the insects, bumper stickers featuring the motto "Blood Donor," fly swatters, and T-shirts were all emblazoned with the logo of The Official Greenhead Swat Team.

We started assembling our booth on a busy, brick pedestrian mall where the likelihood of high foot traffic seemed most promising, and before we had completed the task of setting up, we had already attracted a small crowd. Our khaki uniforms, white pith helmets and large "Official Greenhead Swat Team" banner caused onlookers to stop to determine what had possessed such apparently well-meaning but misguided folks to glorify the dreaded seasonal infestation. Seeing that the whole thing was a spoof, most found it easy to temporarily set aside their disdain for the pesky insects and, for one day at least, see them as the cute and endearing caricatures that our logo suggested. Some even reached for their wallets, displaying a momentary affinity for the cute little creatures by purchasing one or two tokens of our temporary affinity for them. We took in so much money, in fact, that by day's end we came close to actually covering our modest expenses, nearly jeopardizing our status as a non-profit enterprise. While breaking even or turning a small profit would have been a pleasant surprise, our purpose was not to make a few dollars as much as it was to make a few people smile. By that measure, the team accomplished its modest mission.

Each July, the greenheads arrive on schedule to terrorize seacoast residents, bringing with them a few short weeks of pain, inconvenience, and irritation. For a few of us, however, they also bring renewed memories of mock celebration as members of the short-lived Official Greenhead Swat Team. And even as we attempt to swat the persistent pests that tear our flesh and make us grimace, we do so remembering the day they also made us smile.

Playing With Fire

I stand before the campfire my Dad has made to allow us kids to toast marshmallows. I carefully position mine over the embers close enough to watch the soft, white confection impaled at the end of my stick turn a golden brown, but not so close that it would actually catch on fire. I had watched my younger sister carelessly hold her anticipated treat too close only to see it erupt into a raging ball of liquid fire. I proudly demonstrate the proper technique, explaining that the exact distance above the glowing embers is critical to yielding a well-crafted, perfectly prepared delicacy.

Just as I'm smugly flaunting my expertise, the marshmallow at the end of my stick bursts into flames. Attempting to make a quick recovery, I yank it back from the campfire to avert an embarrassing failure only to have the flaming projectile land with a sugary splat on top of my bare foot.

I don't remember if my sister commented or simply laughed at the sound of my scream. I remember only the severe pain as the melting residue seared my skin leaving a red and blistery welt that remained for days as a reminder of my carelessness. It was a lesson shamefully learned as a ten-year-old about the effects of hot fire coming into contact with skin.

Fast forward thirty-two years. Once again I find myself standing before another fire on a beautiful, warm evening. The Danvers Fire Department is busy tending the fire that they themselves have set. The cords of hardwood set ablaze only hours before has now reached the point at which it is ready to be raked into a twelve-foot long bed of glowing embers. Carefully smoothed to conform to the dimensions of the pre-made fire pit, the coals radiate a blistering heat of approximately one thousand degrees Fahrenheit.

The sun has set and in the nearby parking lot a crowd of curious bystanders gather to witness a truly remarkable phenomenon. In the growing darkness, the embers pulsate with glowing orange ferocity. I can feel the searing heat scalding my shins as I stand at the edge of the pit.

It seemed improbable that were I to step onto this fire with my bare feet that it would not result in the same severe burns and blistering I had encountered years earlier. Logic would dictate that fire is fire. And fire burns human skin. My own experience had proven that to be true. Yet I was now being told that, perhaps, this was not always the case. I was being asked to suspend my previously held beliefs and consider the possibility that stepping onto this fire with my bare feet might not have the same effect that it did decades ago.

But why should this be so? My feet had changed little in the intervening years. Other than growing a few sizes, they were virtually identical to those that had transported me through my childhood. But that is precisely why I was intrigued enough to participate in this bizarre ritual.

Humans the world over have been doing this for thousands of years, the earliest known reference having occurred in India about the year 1200 BC. If everyone who walked across fire ended up with third-degree burns, I rationalized, people would not continue to undergo such voluntary torture.

For several hours this evening, I had been learning about this ancient custom from Doctor Hart, who first studied this practice in India. As he lectured approximately twenty willing participants in a room adjacent to where the fire awaited, he assured us that if we followed his instructions, we'd be able to walk the length of the fire pit totally unaffected by what we were walking on. He further explained that, although the fire would reach temperatures nearly double the melting point of lead, we should trust that he would not let any of us spontaneously combust. The disturbing thought of my sister's marshmallow came to mind, but he assured us that he would be right there beside us next to the fire pit.

"*Beside us?*" I asked skeptically. "Are you not going to walk with us over the fire?"

Doctor Hart insisted we would get more out of what we were to undertake if we went alone into the fire—that he would walk beside us the length of the fire, but outside of the actual pit.

This prompted several in the group to ask, "Are you sure you've done this before?" Doctor Hart's silent smile was meant to reassure us, but left some beginning to question their own judgment and the image of my sister's incinerated marshmallow again came to mind.

As Doctor Hart continued to instruct the group, he led us in a group meditation in which we imagined the hot coals to be a bed of cool, soft snow. Envisioned with enough conviction, he insisted, we would begin to believe it and this would eventually become our reality. Had this feat never been performed before, we might have believed it to be physically impossible. We might have relied upon past evidence that fire burns human skin. After all, we had been taught since childhood not to touch a hot stove. But we'd also heard about people in India and other places walking across fire with no ill effects. Was this some kind of trick photography? Some sort of deliberate deception?

The meditation through which our instructor led us was designed to instill in our minds an altered belief of the potential effect of fire on our bare feet. This perception-altering exercise was to prove to us that what we perceive in our minds has real-life effects—that it's not just make believe. Doctor Hart explained that the human mind is so powerful that it's actually capable of changing our reality.

Before the hours-long preparation was to come to an end, our confident instructor asked each of us to identify our biggest fear as we pondered the feat we were about to undertake. The fears expressed by the group ranged from being burned alive to being embarrassed if we were to chicken out at the last minute. Doctor Hart then had us write our fears on a piece of paper and crumple it into a fist-size ball. Having obediently done so, we were led out to pay our respects to the awaiting fire. We lined up along the edge of the sweltering inferno, and on command, tossed our papers into the fire. Before my paper had even touched the coals, it ignited in a ball of flame like an ill-fated marshmallow on the end of a stick held too close to the fire.

Doctor Hart then led us in a group chant of *"Cool, soft*

snow. Cool, soft snow" which could be heard throughout the parking lot next to where we were about to test the boundaries of our new-found beliefs. The key to successfully performing this feat, he insisted, was to embody the deep-seated faith that it could actually be done. In other words, if we truly believed it, this would become our reality.

One by one, standing at the end of the fire pit, our instructor held our wrists and gave us one final word of encouragement. He reminded each of us to walk slowly as we crossed the embers. He had earlier warned us that if we were to walk too quickly, we would be tempting fate and would likely get burned. This, he explained, is because moving too quickly over the fire is an indication that we do not thoroughly believe we can do this. It is an indication that our brain is sub-consciously receiving signals telling it *"I'd better hurry or I'll get burned."* If there remains any doubt in our mind about the outcome, all bets are off. Those who attempt such a feat with no mental preparation are almost guaranteed to be severely injured.

When the moment came and our instructor sensed that we were ready to take that big first step, we did so while firm-ly holding the perception that we were walking on cool, soft snow. We were assured that if we focused on that belief, we would remain unburned and unharmed, yet unquestionably altered.

When my turn arrived, I confidently stepped up to the end of the fire pit. Doctor Hart held my wrist and looked directly into my eyes. His extensive training allowed him to sense any hint of doubt yet remaining. It was not until he was certain I was ready, that he nodded, giving me the signal that I could take my first step. At that point, I was free to walk, although I could still decide not to. It was my choice.

May 24, 1989. The author takes a big step.

Without hesitation, I stepped onto the bed of hot coals as my fellow participants encouraged and supported me with a continuous chant of *"Cool, soft snow."* Under the weight of my body I felt the burning coals press against the bottoms of my bare feet as they sank slightly into the unstable surface. With each step the glowing embers shifted under the pressure of my feet. But there was not the slightest sensation of heat. The uneven texture was what I imagined it might feel like to walk across a bed of popcorn.

As I approached the end of the fire pit, what was in reality just a short walk, suddenly took on epic proportions. The new-found power I felt in that moment has stayed with me these many years, as I am often reminded of the mind's ability to bend our so-called "reality" and to transform what we believe to be true. It has kept me from placing artificial limits on possible outcomes simply because I believed them to be improbable. My initial skepticism about participating in this questionable ritual was overruled by a deep faith in possibility.

In the end, I'm grateful that I listened to that inner voice nudging me to take a chance. I'm just glad I didn't chicken out and get "cold feet."

Well, no chance of that I guess.

Why I'm Running for President

To an outsider, it may seem like a far-fetched idea. But to anyone who knows me, it's completely insane. But hear me out.

In looking back during my lifetime at what Presidents have done, it seems that almost all of the major events and decisions involving the country have been made not by the President, but by those attending to him. Consultants, department heads, ambassadors, Generals, and other experts as well as the Congress have been largely responsible for virtually all of the recommendations acted upon by the government. The President has been informed, sometimes at the last minute, about information leading to actions taken by the military, the Senate, the healthcare system, national security, and so on. These actions seem to come from the President, but they really originate with those who surround him.

Do you think when mid-west farmers lose thirty-two percent of revenue due to drought conditions compounded by a precipitous drop in wheat prices because of tariffs placed on it by China, that it's the President who makes an in-depth study of all the pros and cons of possible actions and their ramifications? Do you think it's the President who's diligence and proactive analysis makes the determination to counter by placing a twelve percent tariff on imported steel, and then using the added revenue to provide a six-hundred eighty-two million dollar subsidy to the wheat farmers? Really? You think it's the President who figures this out?

Whether it's an expert on banking, the environment, infrastructure, transportation, or foreign trade policy, there are government officials steeped in their particular fields of expertise. They spend every hour of every day studying the data to determine what policies are in the best interest of the country. They then report to the President or sometimes just to his staff. No one person can be expected to know all there is to know about everything. No one has enough intelligence, let alone enough time, to be completely knowledgeable about every subject important to an entire country. If this were the case, not only would a President never have time to golf, but he would probably never find the time to eat a meal or sleep.

Because of our government's system of checks and balances, in actuality, there's very little a President can do on his own. He can't make laws, he can't declare war. He can't even determine trade policy with other countries. Those decisions are up to the Congress and the Senate. He can nominate judges, but that's as far as it goes. Their confirmation is up to the Senate. The President's nominees are taken merely as suggestions, nothing more.

If I am elected, as President, I will from time to time, suggest, request, or even insist that the Congress consider laws I believe are necessary. But it's the Congress that makes the final decision. I can let people know what my views are on various topics and suggest actions, but ultimately, it's up to other branches of government to find a way to enact my suggestions or not. As long as there are highly qualified individuals judging my ideas as good or bad, I'm willing, if elected, to make those suggestions every so often as they occur to me. But mostly, I'll stand back and let the experts in each department decide what needs to be done, and then let me know.

In all, there are fifteen executive departments that carry out the day-to-day administration of the federal government, all of which need constant oversight. But even this oversight isn't the President's job. That's what a President's Cabinet is for. It's these hard-working individuals in various departments who do the heavy lifting for which the President takes a bow and accepts all the credit. It's the Cabinet and these independent federal agencies that are responsible for the day-to-day enforcement and administration of federal laws.

These agencies and departments include the Department of Defense, the CIA, the Environmental Protection Agency, the Social Security Administration, and the Securities and Exchange Commission. While not part of the Cabinet, they do have the responsibility to make policy and decide the best course of action for the country. As is the case with the Cabinet as well as the heads of some of these other agencies, the President can fire them if he doesn't like what they recommend. However, that still doesn't mean he can simply do as he likes. He can hire another department head hoping that person will make decisions he likes better, but the President is obliged to follow their advice. When the President hears something he thinks will make people like him, he tells the department head, "Yeah. Let's do that."

People may think the President is responsible for all this, but when it comes right down to it, he's just a temporary employee living in subsidized public housing and, if he's smart, following the specific advice given him by these many agencies. If elected, I promise, as has been the tradition, to simply do what is recommended by my experts and take the credit.

Besides hiring and firing his Cabinet, a few other things a President can do entirely on his own include the dubious ability to pardon convicted felons. This he can do with no recourse for those who disagree. He can also hire and fire individual members of his immediate staff such as his Press Secretary, Ambassadors, department heads, and so on. Often, these positions have little or no bearing on real-world consequences, and many Americans would be hard-pressed to name the individuals holding these important positions.

Under Article II of the Constitution, the President is also responsible for the enforcement of the laws created by Congress. In other words, he gets to tell people to do what they're already supposed to do by law. If elected, I think I would be quite capable of telling people to obey the law.

So it is only after careful consideration that I announce my candidacy for President of the United States. It is after thoughtful analysis that I take this monumental step. I also do so with the utmost humility and the sacred promise to surround myself with experts on all topics that effect the lives and well-being of the fine people of this great country. I'll recruit the best Generals, scientists, and comedy writers. Trust me, you'll be in very good hands. Having fulfilled all three of the necessary legal qualifications for this important position—

being born in The United States, being at least thirty-five years of age, and having lived in this country for at least fourteen years—I am ready to assume the position of Commander-in-Chief. I hereby promise to sit back, look important, and do whatever my most qualified advisers tell me I should do. Although it's a position that looks important, in reality it's mostly symbolic. I believe I'm up to the task.

Many citizens listen to the President and think it's the President himself who is making all those grandiose statements, when in fact, he's just repeating the well-chosen words of his trusted advisors as he reads from the teleprompter. If I'm elected I believe I can be relied upon to do just that. I'm a very good reader.

At times, a President might think he knows better than the experts. The lawmakers in Congress, for example, who actually do the work of researching and debating an issue write a proposed law and send it to the President's desk. This happens only after long, in-depth discussions and debate that can take months. The President then has a very important job. He picks up a ballpoint pen (usually in front of cameras) and writes his name on a piece of paper. He then gets to claim credit for enacting a new law. Occasionally, however, when the President doesn't like what's placed in front of him, and thinks he knows better than the career experts, he can choose to veto the bill. This is the equivalent of giving a thumbs down by writing his name on a different piece of paper.

Even the President's veto, however, can be challenged and thrown out by the very people who proposed the law. All the Congress needs to do is have two thirds of their members say "no" to the President and inform him that "we want this to become law. That's why we gave you that piece of paper to sign in the first place."

If elected, I promise to listen to the people who have been elected to propose legislation that they believe should become law. It would be presumptuous of me, for example, to override their well-informed decision to designate the Northern Leopard Frog as the official amphibian of The United States.

I will come to the office of the Presidency with the humble awareness that I am your public servant in whom you can trust to fulfill all of the symbolic acts that are a President's sacred duty to perform. I will at all times keep a ballpoint pen at my side in case I am presented with a piece of paper on which I am to write my name thus displaying my unwavering agreement with the experts who know more than me.

I will, however, assume the Presidency with my own ideas for making this great country even better. I have pondered these ideas with great sincerity and debated in my own mind their effects on the country.

For example, to ease race relations, I'll remove the word "white" from "The White House" and rename it simply "The House." After centuries of inequality and prejudice against black people, that should calm things down a bit. You're welcome.

I will also suggest that the United States end the wasteful production of pennies. After learning that it costs the mint more than two cents to make a one-cent piece, I will propose we finally put a stop to this shockingly outrageous waste of precious resources. This alone could end the deficit and balance the federal budget.

Another money-saving idea is to put an end to the millions of dollars we spend each year for the storage of federal property that is no longer being used. Government warehouses are packed with everything from furniture, books, vehicles, computers, and even personal articles once used by former Presidents. No law currently exists for the disposal of this property. Under my administration the Federal Government will set up an eBay account to not only purge these unused articles, but to also make money on their sale by allowing private citizens to own a piece of history. Citizens will now have the unique opportunity to own a toothbrush once used by Woodrow Wilson, or the Bible President Reagan used to swat flies in the Lincoln bedroom. This, combined with the "no-penny" policy could also help reduce the need for income taxes.

And while we're at it, we don't need some fancy Secretary-of-State to whom we pay an obscenely high salary. I know a woman at the company I once worked for who was a wonderful secretary. Irene could type sixty-five words a minute and was great at taking notes. I'm sure if I asked her nicely, she'd consider becoming a secretary again.

Yeah, all these ideas may not prevent nuclear war, stop the threat of global warming, or an imbalance in trade policy. But I'll have experts for that.

I'm David Random, and I approved this message.

Brimfield

I held the fragile, glass vacuum tube in my hands, carefully examining the structure for any sign of damage. Holding the vintage relic up to the light, I peered into its intricate interior, marveling at the technology of yesteryear. At nearly eighteen inches long, I had never seen one approaching such staggering proportion.

"How much?" I asked.

"Thirty-five dollars," the man replied, adding that he wasn't sure if it still worked.

"I'll give you twenty," I countered. "And I don't care if it works."

"What are you going to do with it then?"

"It's going into a rocketship."

I had deliberately not provided any explanation or details because I enjoy watching people's reaction when they hear my pat answer to the question I get all the time. Occasionally, if someone shows enough curiosity, I elaborate on my unique hobby of creating rocketship sculptures from antique and vintage artifacts. I occasionally give them one of my cards with photos and watch their puzzled expression morph into one of amused delight as they begin to identify components re-imagined from their original purpose. It might be a garden hose nozzle, an old flashlight, or a vintage fire extinguisher. Sometimes it might be parts from a kerosene lamp, clock movements, or old TV antennas.

He scowls at me thinking I had been making fun of him.

"Thirty is as low as I'll go," he says.

"Okay, thanks." I carefully replace the fragile artifact on the table in front of him as I turn to slowly walk away, allowing sufficient time for him to rethink and accept my offer. I stop at the next booth and glance back waiting for a counter offer to what I thought was a reasonable sum to pay for a glass vacuum tube that doesn't work. He's already busy helping another customer. So I move on.

The massive glass vacuum tube was larger than any I had ever seen. I was determined not to leave without it.

Today I was scouring the Brimfield Flea Market in Brimfield, Massachusetts. Considered America's oldest outdoor antiques market, Brimfield has been drawing dealers and shoppers for over fifty years. Three times a year for a week at a time this small rural town is transformed into a sprawling mecca for antique shoppers as thousands of dealers offer their wares in fields that spread across an area so vast that one would have to view it from a helicopter to grasp its full extent.

As I wind my way through the seemingly endless rows of dealers trying not to retrace my previous course, I search out other antique and vintage artifacts to be repurposed as rocket parts. For years I have fashioned these flea market finds into the "retro rockets" for which I have become widely known. I happen upon one booth with a vast array of glass telephone pole insulators. I already have several in my studio, but this particular collection features several in colors I do not have. And the price is right—three dollars each. I don't even barter with the dealer. I pay the man and throw a couple into my backpack.

Lunch time arrives and I've already made one trip back to my car to unload the morning's purchases—an antique wooden newel post, a hood ornament from an old Buick, a beautiful pair of old brass opera glasses, and several vintage kitchen utensils. These pieces will eventually become components of rocketships that, hopefully, will find their way into the art galleries and museums that feature my work.

Because many of the dealers here at Brimfield are perpetual participants, and because in many cases, they tend to occupy the same spaces year after year, I am able to be quite efficient with my time. I know which sections of which fields tend to feature the types of antiques needed for my rocketships. I also know which sections I am able to quickly skim or avoid altogether. I'm not interested in the antique furniture in which some dealers specialize. And I scurry past booths that seem to have a lot of high-priced vintage glassware or antique quilts and old Life Magazines. I search instead for those vestiges of bygone eras that maintain their original shape and finish that I can conceivably repurpose.

From vintage egg beaters and bicycle pedals to old sewing machine parts, the shapes and finishes of these obsolete elements combine to take on new life as fantasy vessels to be launched into space in one's imagination. Most pieces will not find their alternate purpose immediately. The majority will find a place in my studio where they will wait until the appropriate time when other relics present themselves to be combined as one cohesive unit.

Combining parts requires special attention to the details of conformity. For this to happen, several things must fall into place. First, the shapes must fit together to create a believable unit. The shape of each individual component must blend with others as if they had been made to conform. Together, they must maintain an integrity that allows one's imagination to see it as something designed with a single aesthetic and purpose. Although the different elements should remain identifiable, the finished creation cannot look like a patchwork quilt.

Conformity also goes beyond just the shape of a component. The material has to be compatible as well. If a sculpture includes a lot of beautifully tarnished brass, I can't just throw in a piece of silver, even if the shape is perfect. The whole credibility of the finished creation would go out the window with that type of inconsistency.

This conformity also pertains to the age of the individual pieces. This means, for example, that a component from the 1950s would be out of place if combined with one from the 1890s. When components need to be fastened by means of screws or bolts I go to my stash of salvaged fasteners. It would destroy the effect of a finished piece to use new hardware to fasten antique pieces.

As I continue my treasure hunt I pass other shoppers clutching their precious finds. Some carry old movie posters, lamps, and candlesticks. Others have found vintage clothing, clocks, and books. Some see my purchases as I pass and I'm sure they wonder why anyone would want a broker vacuum cleaner or the bottom half of a old hair dryer.

As the end of the day draws near, dealers begin to pack up until the following day when they will once again spread their wares before an enthralled public. I'm nearing the exit to one of the many fields and notice that the man with the glass vacuum tube is still there. I nonchalantly wander in his direction until I'm close enough to see the huge vacuum tube still sitting at the end of one of his tables. This time I don't stop to pick it up. Instead, I point to it as I pass without stopping to show interest.

"Twenty dollars," I say as I'm almost past his booth.

Out of the corner of my eye I see him take a deep breath. "Okay, twenty," he grudgingly concedes. Recalling our conversation of several hours ago, he quips in a decidedly mocking tone, "The rocketship, right?"

He carefully wraps the piece in newspaper, and I hand over a twenty-dollar bill. As I gently load it into my backpack, I smile and thank the man.

"It really *is* going into a rocketship," I explain. I hand

him a card picturing one of my finished pieces, explaining to him what I do with these odd flea market finds.

He studies my card and hands me one of his own. "I'd love to see it when it's done. Send me a picture."

I agree to do so and head back to my car. I'm two booths away when I look back in his direction. He's still holding my card when he looks up and sees me. Giving me the thumbs up, he yells at the top of his lungs, "Blast off!"

This specialized niche I've found to channel my creativity is one I've been developing for about two decades. My rocketships can now be found in museums and art galleries in the New England area and beyond. They've been featured in magazines, television, and movies. I've found it to be a great pastime that brings me much satisfaction and happiness. And I've found it to be a natural extension of my imagination.

Hey, it's not rocket science.

Well... perhaps.

Two views of the finished rocketship. The piece incorporates additional glass vacuum tubes of smaller sizes, a clear glass telephone pole insulator, a vintage hood ornament, parts from a vintage Thermos bottle, a metal bathroom cup holder, and pegs from a 1950's Lite Brite toy. The entire assembly sits atop a vintage smoking stand base.

There's Always a First Time

I once went for twelve years without showering. This questionable accomplishment came about not due to a lack of hygiene, but rather, a lack of plumbing. You see, as a kid, none of the homes in which we lived ever had anything as luxurious as a shower. What we had instead, were bulky, white tubs in which I soaked every Saturday night, marinating in my own dingy water.

Most of the tubs I remember were held slightly above the floor on big iron feet in the shape of eagles' talons—a symbolic imagery that added a ceremonial feeling to the weekly ritual. These adornments were a carry-over from an earlier time when such embellishments were considered fashionable. This was, no doubt, someone's questionable attempt to make bath time somehow more stylish. It is probable that some of our tubs were original relics dating from that era, as many of my childhood homes were of considerable antiquity.

One large, Victorian house where I lived in Boston had been home to several generations of my family dating back to my great-grandparents. The tub that regularly supported the unwashed backsides of my ancestors features prominently in my mother's childhood recollections. On bath night, she recalls, a succession of family members would soak in the same bath water, beginning with the cleanest, followed by those who were less so. It would not be until the filthiest child (often a toddler who had been crawling around on the floor) had dissolved away the layers of grime, that the chain on the big rubber plug was finally pulled, allowing the gray liquid to slowly gurgle its way to what my older cousin had once informed me was the ocean. By the time the last child had bathed, the water was usually so dirty that you could barely see into it. It was this tradition of bathing hierarchy, common in many households, that led to the expression "don't throw the baby out with the bath water."

It wasn't until seventh grade gym class that I finally took my first shower. Until that time, I could only imagine what it might be like to stand beneath a glorious stream of hot water rushing full force over my body. Actually, my adolescent modesty prevented me from thoroughly enjoying my initial indoctrination. I was more conscious of the fact that I was standing in the midst of twenty other naked students, and Kenneth Moyer was snapping his wet towel at me. It also ended much too quickly, as Mr. Boylen, our gym teacher, found great enjoyment in adjusting the master shower controls to produce a rush of cold water after only a few short minutes of well-deserved indulgence, thus precipitating a panicky mass exit. By all measure, my first shower was a disappointment when compared with expectations.

There's a first time for everything. Our lives are a series of firsts. Some are remembered as life-changing milestones by which we measure happiness, age, success—incredibly meaningful events that make indelible impressions on our lives. Your first kiss, your first job, your first trip on an airplane all fall into this important category. Other firsts leave disproportionate impressions since, as events go, they are essentially meaningless.

I remember the first time I put a worm on a fish hook by myself, yet I have no recollection of my first day of school. I remember my first taste of Swiss cheese, but I don't recall my first day of employment. I vividly remember the first time I played with a yo-yo. But I can barely remember the make and model of my first car.

Memories of various "first time" occurrences clutter my mind with no apparent order of importance. Life-changing events are crammed together with those that are totally irrelevant. Sometimes it seems the less consequential a first-time event is, the more it adamantly sticks with us. The first time I ate snow, saw a live chicken, and first used Velcro are all permanently and indelibly set in my mind. Yet over the years, I expect the need to recall them will probably seldom arise.

Other firsts I have no recollection of, but trust they actually happened only because they are preserved for eternity and memorialized in family albums. My first necktie is one such forgettable event, followed by my first attempt at sideburns.

Some firsts are also "only"s—the first and only time I stuck my finger in that light socket, the first and only time I ate a cricket mistaking it for a toasted walnut. The first and only time I ate a cricket actually knowing what it was. (In all fairness, it *was* covered with chocolate.)

There are many firsts, some good and some bad, that

are unique to our individual lives. Those are the firsts that, for one reason or another, others may never get a chance to experience. The places we've traveled, the sights we've seen, and the things we've done may all fall into this category. We may think ourselves lucky to have experienced these firsts. Others, not so much. However they are judged, every life is a succession of firsts that bring us to this present moment. Without these firsts, our lives would be, by definition, a series of repeats—a sequence of familiar events characterized by predictability. Without the prospect of another first, we would, no doubt, find life rather boring.

So whenever you find yourself stuck in the same old pattern, whenever you find yourself thinking, *"Here we go again,"* take a deep breath and embrace new possibilities. Get out there and try something new.

An Owners Manual for Humans

I have long felt that something as complicated as a human being should come with a comprehensive owners manual. Tucked away in the glove compartment of my car is an owners manual so thick that it could be used as a booster seat for children. In it, every conceivable component, function, and problem with my car is addressed. My computer and cell phone each came with a bulky manual outlining not only instructions for use, but tips on how to spy on my neighbors. Even my electric toothbrush came with a sizable instruction booklet.

So after the birth of a newborn baby, why should it be that parents—especially the first-timers—are sent home with nothing more than a "good-luck" wave and a hefty bill. Surely a tiny human needs more care and maintenance than a toothbrush. Yet, here we are. Every day there are about eleven thousand births in The United States, many of them to first-time parents. So in an effort to provide much needed instructions as to the care, feeding, and scheduled maintenance of this vast onslaught of new human beings, I have taken it upon myself to create the long-overdue "Owners Manual for Humans."

Attached for your convenience are a few excerpts from this first-of-its-kind manual designed to provide many years of trouble-free performance for its owners. Please be advised that the information contained herein is solely the express opinions and unproven advise of the author. Results may vary.

Introduction: Congratulations on your decision to acquire a brand new human. If you did not choose this and your ownership came as a surprise, tough! You will still be happy to know that the accompanying manual will provide you with detailed and necessary instructions designed to help you navigate the many years of rewarding, and at times, confusing scenarios you will undoubtedly encounter as a new parent. Whether you have acquired the M-model or the F-model, you will find that much of the information contained herein applies to both models with little distinction. If this is not the first human you have acquired, repeat the same steps as with previous humans, except this time, do not let it roam freely around the house with a box of finger paints or feed the dog crayons.

Although your new human comes with no factory warranty, rest assured it has been carefully inspected for damage before wrapping it up and sending it with you on your merry way. Regular scheduled maintenance as outlined in this manual is recommended to ensure many years of trouble-free ownership, after which you may choose to safely release your human into the wild. This, however, is recommended only after successfully witnessing its ability to pick up its toys and safely cross the street, although it may periodically return without warning carrying dirty laundry and asking for money.

Diapers: This optional equipment may be purchased at any drug store or baby human supply depot. Diapers come in a range of sizes, materials, and strengths. From time to time (actually, nearly *all* the time) you will find that your human will leak fluids and other disturbing substances from the two holes located mid-body at the front and the rear of your human. This is quite normal and should not be seen as a sign of malfunction. When this happens, check to see if the equipment needs changing. This may be done simply by picking up your human and holding it in front of your face. Then, making certain your grip is secure, inhale deeply. If you are met with any aroma other than talcum powder, please see the section on diaper changing located on page 62 of this manual.

Special note to fathers: Do not use a diaper as a bib, especially after it has been soiled. This will not only result in your new human's lasting distaste for apple sauce, but will undoubtedly cause your wife to severely reprimand you.

Refueling: (also known as feeding) During the first year or so of ownership, special fuel is available—and, in fact necessary—for your human. Until your new human has learned to run on regular fuel, it is recommended that you use only fuels specifically made for humans of this young age during the breaking-in period. This special fuel may be found in most grocery stores in a section labeled "infant and baby needs." For best results, you will want to use only premium and unleaded fuels. You will recognize these highly specific fuels by their tiny, glass jars and their hugely large price. These fuels generally consist of various fruit and vegetables that have been pureed beyond recognition except for their color. Please refer to the words on the label for specific contents. Despite their near liquid consistency, these fuels should be given orally, and are not meant to be injected by means of hypodermic needles. Due to the small scale of your brand new human, quantities of fuel should be adjusted accordingly. Please be advised that it is not recommended to feed your human adult-size portions large enough to fill a huge soup bowl, as this may cause a back-up of fuel to be redistributed onto your shirt. An automatic warning indicator comes built in to your new human. You will know when you are in danger of over-fueling when your human turns its head away from an oncoming spoonful of fuel, or when he or she pushes the entire dish of pureed beets onto the floor. This may sometimes occur simply because you are trying to feed it pureed beets.

Gradually, you may attempt to provide your new human with so-called adult fuel provided that care is taken to ensure that it is of soft consistency such as bananas or oatmeal. (It is advised that bananas be removed from their peels prior to feeding. Please refrain from using dog treats and make certain that oysters on the half shell have been thoroughly removed from their shells.)

Special note: The use of kale and brussels sprouts should definitely be restricted and not attempted until such time as your human can voice disapproval in a way that does not involve crying or throwing food at a nearby wall.

Replacement parts: Generally speaking, replacement parts are not available for your new human. Exceptions to this include teeth (for which one set is included at no additional cost), hair, and the occasional finger or toe nail. (That's *finger nail*, not *finger*.) Care should be taken to protect all parts from damage by proper supervision until such time as your human demonstrates an ability to stand on its own and to walk without falling into the gutter. Occasionally, your human may revert to this behavior after it has already passed the "walk on its own" test. If such behavior should occur after this developmental milestone, please refer to the section on use of alcohol.

Optional equipment: Certain additional equipment may be purchased for use with your new human for the purpose of demonstrating your newly-acquired parenting skills or showing off your wealth. These may range from expensive, designer car seats complete with built-in cup holders, massaging seat, and video player, to overly-fancy strollers. Owners of the F-model human may at some point wish to consider pierced ears with small studs as optional equipment for their young F-model human to demonstrate their fashion sense. This, however, is not recommended for ages prior to six weeks. Owners may also want to eventually consider pierced ears for their M-model as a way to demonstrate their open-mindedness.

Some owners may also want to consider the addition of cute hats, brightly-colored booties, one-piece suits ("one-zies"), and pajamas featuring colorful cartoon characters as a way to enhance their enjoyment. (Warning: This may cause complete strangers to stop and coo or overtly wave to your little human who will probably show little or no interest.)

Safety precautions: It is recommended that appropriate safety measures be taken at all times. These may include, but are not limited to, hand holding when crossing streets and parking lots, keeping your new human away from chainsaws and other power equipment until they understand the word "no", covering its ears when Family Guy is on TV, and strapping into an approved children's car seat when riding in an automobile. (Note: when strapping into a car seat, place human in a sitting position with front of human facing out, head at top and feet at bottom extending forward. Tighten restraining belts until breathing becomes labored, then loosen slightly before driving.)

Snooze control: Owners may find from time to time that your small human wakes up repeatedly during the night and cries. Often this is quite temporary and, if left alone, will quickly resolve itself with no involvement by the owner. Sometimes, however, these disturbances may be quite prolonged. If this should happen, there are a number of steps owners may take to remedy the situation.

1.) Sing a soft lullaby in the vicinity of your human while occasionally stroking its back.

2.) Play soothing music for your new human to hear, but at a low volume. (Avoid at all costs, however, playing anything by Snoop Dog, Chance The Rapper, Beastie Boys, or Jay-Z.)

3.) Put a headset on and listen to the music yourself, blocking out all other ambient sound.

4.) Disturbances during the night may also be mitigated by feeding your human warm milk just before bedtime. If that remedy fails, feeding yourself tequila or whiskey just before bedtime has also been shown to have positive results.

Automatic maintenance indicator: Your brand new human comes with a built-in automatic indicator warning system that will alert you if something goes wrong (and it will). The warning alert will come in the form of loud crying or screaming. This is an indication that something is wrong and that you perhaps should stop trying to stuff your new human into a one-piece snowsuit, or force it to remain in the shopping cart while at the supermarket, or that you have left him or her out in the rain.

In summary: While there are some basic differences between the standard equipment on the M- and F- models of human being, many of these differences will not show up for approximately twelve years, at which time you may choose to avail yourself of our 4,250-page "Owners Manual and Trouble Shooting Guide for Adolescents" which may be purchased from the author for two installments of $45,000.

The Do-Over

I've decided after many decades to grant myself a do-over. By my own rules, I allow myself a re-do of any event in my life that I deem unworthy of my high esteem and superior regard. My rules are simple. I get to access an event of my own choosing by traveling back in time and doing a re-set of history, allowing myself another chance to make good by altering the memory of the outcome.

Now, I know what you're thinking. Actually, I don't, but if I were you I'd be thinking, *Hey, you can't just pick an event in your past and re-do it, hoping for a better outcome.* If I were you I'd also be thinking, *Hey, that sounds good. Why don't you go back and pick winning lottery numbers.*

First of all, it doesn't work that way. My official rules for a do-over specifically state that when I go back in time, I do not have access to information about anything that occurred after that exact moment. That means that I wouldn't know what the winning lottery numbers were to be. Were that the case, I could also choose to invest large sums of money in Apple or Microsoft stock at a time when no one had ever heard of them. I could also, for that matter, choose *not* to invest in that company that made that tuna-flavored ice cream. (Who knew that would never catch on.) Furthermore, I'm not changing the actual event, just my memory of it.

No, the way it works is that I get to choose any moment in my past, and without knowing any more than I did at that exact time, I hit "re-set" on the clock of history. Then, I get to live that moment again in my mind, hoping for a different outcome. For some reason, the one moment I always choose to re-do is one that occurred way back when I was twelve. That moment would undoubtedly have long faded from memory were it not for the fact that my mother saved a clipping from our local newspaper emblazoning the event in my mind whenever my eyes happen to fall upon it as I browse through the family scrapbook. I've all but forgotten about the dubious occurrence until... WHAM! There it is staring me in the face, headline reaching out in bold type, "Random Pitches One Hitter." Then, I can't get it out of my mind—the fact that I came so close to being perfect. So close! I know if I could just have one more go at it the outcome would be much more satisfying.

I was the star pitcher for the Tigers and I had a perfect game going. Every time I'd return to the dugout between innings, my teammates would slap me on the back, commenting on my performance with accolades like, "Wow, you've got a no-hitter going." and "Hey, Dave, just two more innings and you've done it!"

Then it happened. I don't know whether I became too casual, too confident or what, but I know if I could just go back to that day, back to the mound and focus a little more on the job at hand, I could change what the newspaper report claims actually happened. It was that guy, Snyder, as the newspaper clipping states, who hit, not a little dribbling ground ball for a weak single, but a rocket off the outfield fence for a double. Oh, the embarrassment! The disgrace! Sure, we won the game. It was a shutout. And we were in first place in the league. But the unsettling truth has haunted me ever since. Every time I browse through the family scrapbook it's there. I picture Snyder pointing at me and laughing. Ridiculing me. A do-over would be all that's needed to put him in his place.

I'd stare in at that uppity creep from the mound, my perch high above all else on the field. Then I'd give him my famous evil eye, causing him to wither with self-doubt. "Strike one!" the umpire would shout. Smitty, my catcher, would return the ball and I'd confidently stroll back onto the pitching rubber for the next humiliating fast ball to Snyder. "Strike two!" would come the call from the umpire standing in awe of my "superb control" as the newspaper article aptly notes.

Then, with my teammates waving wildly, and the crowd on its feet (and not just because there were no seats at Goward field) I'd plan my final and devastating attack on the unsuspecting Snyder. Staring in at Smitty's big catcher's mitt, I'd collect my thoughts and think, *one final pitch and sports history will be forever altered.* I'd take a deep breath and lean in toward the batter's box. All my players in the field as well as Mr. Humphrey, my manager, would be holding their breath. Even the umpire would be expectantly awaiting the overpowering final pitch of the inning. Snyder would be waving his bat as if to say, "C'mon, you little turd. You think you can handle me? Put it right here and I'll show you how it's done."

Finally, my confidence reaching a crescendo, I'd lean back for my wind-up, raise my left leg, and follow through

Random Pitches One Hitter

ACTON—The Colonial Little League saw an exceptional pitching performance Tuesday night in a game between the Tigers and the Indians at Goward Field.

Pitcher, David Random, pitched a 1 hit, no run ball game for the Tigers. His main asset was superb control, walking only one batter. Only two Indians reached 1st base in the entire game. The only hit was a double off the fence by Snyder.

According to Sam Humphrey, Tiger manager, his team is in rare form and the boys are playing a first class game.

with... Oh my God! It's a change-up. Snyder, expecting another fastball, would be left flat-footed and flailing wildly as the surprising pitch snaps into Smitty's mitt. The crowd goes wild. My teammates from the dugout run out onto the field as the umpire jumps up and yells, "Strike three!!! You're out!" My eyes briefly meet Snyder's who then turns away and slinks back to his dugout, tail between his spindly legs.

My status as a hero would now be forever secured, resulting in town-wide celebrations and perhaps a parade. No longer would I be remembered as that disappointing little kid who came so close only to fail, but rather, as that amazing kid who achieved the highest pinnacle any pitcher could hope to achieve. It is likely that, to this day, August third would still be known as "No-Hitter Day" in the little town of Acton, Massachusetts. Schools would be closed (and not just because it's August.) My contract as a pitcher for the Boston Red Sox would soon become a reality, and the world would now breathe easy knowing that everything finally worked out in the way it was intended thanks to a miraculous, little known initiative— The Do-Over.

Lullaby and Good Nightmare

I was in my car on the way to the grocery store and listening to a radio program hosted by a woman doing research on the connection between babies and their mothers. She spoke about the importance of human touch and how babies deprived of this bonding experience often grow up with a lack of social skills which can put them at a relationship disadvantage for the remainder of their lives.

She also spoke about a baby's response to sound and why babies need to hear the soft strains of their mother's voice as reassurance that they are safe and protected. As an example, she then played what is probably the world's most iconic lullaby.

As I approached an intersection, I relaxed into the comfortable and lilting melody, while being careful not to actually close my eyes as she had suggested. I let out a long breath and pictured a motherly figure, singing in her soft and soothing voice. Suddenly, my eyes widened and I sat forward toward the steering wheel as if I were hearing those familiar words for the first time. *"Rock-a-bye baby in the tree top. When the wind blows the cradle will rock."* Wait! What???

I had heard those sweet lyrics since infancy, but had

never really thought about the circumstances they conveyed. Am I to understand that this mother was so irresponsible that she put her baby in a cradle and then hung it from the top of a tree to let the wind blow it around? Didn't she realize her baby could get hurt? What kind of mother would put her innocent child in such danger? What if the baby fell? What if...

My disturbing thought scenario was abruptly interrupted as the lullaby continued. *"When the bough breaks the cradle will fall, and down will come baby, cradle and all."*

OH! MY! GOD! Why are we singing this to babies just as they're being put to bed? Why are we singing about what can only be described as child abuse? It's a good thing infants can't understand what we're saying aside from "Mama" and "Dada." It's a good thing they don't understand that we're singing to them about their possible death and disfigurement.

Once inside the grocery store, I couldn't stop thinking about what I'd just heard. What is this strangely demonic tradition we have of serenading children with songs that are the stuff of nightmares? Wandering up and down the grocery store aisles, everything my eyes fell upon brought up images of innocent little children falling to death and injury from great heights. Baby squash, baby wipes, crushed pineapple, blood oranges, cracked walnuts, baby back ribs, shredded wheat. In my perverse mind, the supermarket shelves seemed to be stocked with reminders of the myriad ways we sing about the harm that can befall our sweet little children. Especially if we hang them from the top of a tree.

Back in the car, I bit into a Baby Ruth candy bar and tried to think of something more pleasant to take my mind off babies dying. I found myself wondering instead, why every children's song that now came to mind was laden with darkly disturbing lyrics. Lyrics like *"There was an old woman who lived in a shoe. She had so many children she didn't know what to do. She gave them some soup without any bread, then whipped them all soundly and sent them to bed."*

So, let me get this straight. This old woman who had obviously never heard of birth control, sent all of her children to bed after feeding them an inadequate meal and then beating them for no reason.

One after another, lullabies and nursery rhymes came into my mind that spoke of violent and tragic events that we happily sing to children throughout their formative years. Humpty Dumpty could have just as easily climbed down from the wall to go for a ride on his bike without having to sustain life-threatening injuries that were beyond the repair of even all the king's men. And why couldn't Jack and Jill bring that pail of water down the hill and make a nice pot of tea to go with their cookies? Why did Jack have to fall down and break his crown while Jill came tumbling after? Those would have made much better nursery rhymes than having to come to such tragic ends.

The more I tried to think of children's songs and lullabies, the more I was bombarded with other twisted and hellish examples of injury and destruction. One after another, they popped into my mind.

"It's raining, it's pouring, the old man is snoring. He bumped his head on the edge of the bed and he couldn't get up in the morning." Could this poor guy not get up because he was dead? Or was it merely severe head trauma we were singing about to our innocent little babies?

And how about *"There was an old lady who swallowed a fly, I don't know why she swallowed a fly, perhaps she'll die."* And what about *"Lady bug, lady bug, fly away home. Your house is on fire and you're children are gone."* Or how about that farmer's wife who chased three little mice who couldn't even see where they were going, to cut off their tails with a carving knife?

Am I missing a deeper meaning to all these horrid nursery rhymes? Are they simply lessons meant to teach children not to eat insects or be careful not to bump their heads? Couldn't we just have the people in the songs get a tiny bruise on their forehead, or just spit the fly out after they learn it doesn't taste as good as Cheerios? Why do they all have to suffer such horrible deaths?

As soon as I got home I decided to do a little research. Turns out, not only are there no hidden positive meanings or morals to the stories, but there are even more dire messages than I was aware of. *"Ring around the rosie,"* as it turns out, is apparently a lovely children's song about the plague, or "black death" that struck Europe in the 1300s. One of the signs of the deadly disease was a red rash or "rosie." People supposedly kept herbs, or "posies" in their pockets to ward off the sickness. Those who didn't... well, I guess *"We all fall down"* needs no explanation. And if that weren't enough, *"London Bridge is falling down."*

So go to sleep little children. Have a nice rest. Pay no attention to all the horrible death, sickness, and injury we've been singing about to you. Sleep tight, and we'll see you in the morning. That is, if you don't come to a tragic end and not survive the night.

The Year 2019 B.C.

Those ancient years designated by the letters "B.C." were not given that distinction until well after the historic turning point when everything changed. People living during that long-ago era did not know that their times would be hereafter referred to by such a dubious descriptor. In the years leading up to that biblical event, the unsuspecting citizens of the world went about their daily lives completely unaware that they were to witness what history would regard as "earth-changing." Unaware of what was to come, they were not living during years designated by the letters B.C. The designation was assigned by the generations who came after and who saw the need to draw a distinction between the way life was before and after that milestone event in Bethlehem. It was their way of acknowledging the vast contrast between the way things had been and the way things had become.

During those last few years of the final countdown to that fateful year zero, the world had no awareness of the biblical event toward which it was inevitably hurdling. Mary and Joseph were still in their adolescent years and had not yet even started dating. Neither of them had any idea that their names would be written into what was to become the most significant book in history—The Holy Bible. She, being trained by her mother in the domestic arts of cooking, sewing, and babysitting. He, studying as a carpenter's apprentice and going off with his buddies to smoke behind the woodpile and tease the camels.

It would be less than a decade until that fast-approaching biblical event that would change everything. The final countdown to "ground zero" passed quickly as the unsuspecting world went about its business. The little town of Bethlehem, unaware of its future significance, remained an unremarkable village with no notable characteristics. It's handful of residents were oblivious to the fact that their tiny village was to be forever commemorated in the lyrics of celebration songs to be sung every December. And the three wise men, still teenage trouble-makers, were referred to by locals as the three wise guys. It would still be some years before they could actually claim to be all that wise.

The little drummer boy had not yet been born, but even after his entry into the ancient world, his parents would have no idea why he seemed so obsessed with his constant drumming. He would not learn until several years later when he was mysteriously called to a local manger what all his incessant racket had been a rehearsal for.

Then it happened. Everything seemed to magically fall into place that night. A bright star appeared in the sky guiding onlookers to the epicenter of the coming out party. Angels on their migratory route to the French Riviera were interrupted mid-flight and summoned to attend the gathering. And under threat of a local ordinance prohibiting the display of a nativity scene on public property, a local innkeeper was able to fulfill his role in history as he just happened to have an empty stable in which to stage the event.

It was, indeed, a milestone occurrence which would change the planet for thousands of years into the future. It was a turning point that, for future generations, would mark the beginning of the long count upward from the year zero and into a more "modern" era. From that point on, the term "B.C." would be affixed to those years of a more primitive time period which preceded the so-called enlightenment of mankind.

But there was another historic event of biblical proportion waiting in the wings. Civilization, however, would have to wait a very long time to see what fate had in store for the world. It would, in fact, be another two-thousand years before the onslaught of this life-changing occurrence. But when the plague unleashed its full devastating effect in 2020, the entire planet was to feel those effects. The time immediately preceding the dreaded plague would be written into the history books as 2019 B.C., or 2019 "Before COVID."

The year 2019 B.C. would mark the end of an innocent world and the ominous beginning of a totally new way of relating to one another as the year 2020 began. No longer would friends shake hands and chat face to face. Innocent close encounters with others were to be avoided, and the simple act of breathing in the vicinity of others became deadly for many. Even when friends were within earshot, their nose and mouths were obscured by masks. No longer could bystanders eavesdrop, as the practice of lip-reading soon became a lost art. Prior to 2019 B.C. the term "social distancing" had meant snubbing someone on social media or removing them from your Facebook account. Now, it was a unit of measurement previously known as six feet, and not to be encroached upon.

Once 2020 established itself as the new normal, citizens the world over fondly remembered 2019 B.C. as "the good old days" when people could cram themselves onto a packed bus or wait forever in a long line at a crowded McDonald's. No longer could you tell if someone was smiling at you by simply seeing their mouth. Simple things we once took for granted now became fond memories of the past.

Although the hoarding of gold, frankincense and myrrh had long since dissipated, it was replaced by the hoarding of toilet paper which created an artificial shortage as panicked citizens stocked up with a five-year supply. Hand sanitizer was also in short supply which led to people learning how to open doors and operate ATM machines with their elbows.

Even small gatherings were discouraged and business meetings, book clubs, and the like were held using a virtual on-line program called Zoom. This enabled people to talk to each other while live images of all participants in the virtual meeting appeared in small frames on their computer screens. This led to a relaxing of the dress code whereby even serious business people started wearing suits and ties or dressy blouses from the waist up, but remained in their pajama bottoms as they "attended" meetings from their own living rooms.

Now, it may be presumptuous of me to take it upon myself to decree a whole new era in the way time is to be marked prior to the year 2020. And it, in fact, may be premature for anyone to write 2019 B.C. into the history books by comparing it to the momentous biblical event that took place two thousand years before. But although these two world-changing events were very different and were separated by such a vast span of time, there are, nevertheless, similarities. Following each event, the far-reaching ramifications extended across the globe and were felt by nearly everyone regardless of age or social status. And in both cases, as the significance of what was happening became fully realized, people the world over began offering their prayers.

And following each event, the very same outpouring of emotion was heard as people the world over looked to the heavens and loudly proclaimed, "Holy Christ!"

The Art of the Fail

Alison's uneasiness was on full display as her new boyfriend slowly picked up the large knife in one hand, and looked toward her as she sat nervously beside him. The family had just gathered around the table for a nice holiday meal and for many of us, this was our first opportunity to meet Jason. He had been dating my sister-in-law for only a short time and she was anxious to impress him with her untested culinary skills. He eyed her loaf of homemade bread expectantly and positioned the knife on the crusty top as he prepared to cut the first slice from one end.

Having carried the results of Alison's novice baking experiment from the kitchen to the dining room table, I was well aware of the extreme effort it might take to saw through the dense and heavy structure, and I awaited what was about to happen with perverse anticipation.

It took no more than a second or two for Jason's expression to turn from joyful anticipation to one of puzzled concern. Given that no chainsaw was readily available, he was left to continue with his demolition project, and he stood up to gain better leverage. Jason feigned a smile when he realized that all eyes were upon him, and continued as if he were sawing through an oak log encased in a turtle shell. Embarrassed, Alison took a bite of mashed potato and pretended not to have noticed the ongoing struggle.

Having witnessed Jason's courageous battle to extricate a slice of the dense material from the end of the loaf, no one else at the table was brave enough (or hungry enough) to attempt to duplicate his bread battle. For the rest of the meal, the remainder of Alison's failed effort remained conspicuously on the table next to the festive holiday bouquet as if it were part of the centerpiece.

Immediately following the lavish meal, I helped clear the table, making sure to set aside Alison's now infamous bread. The heavy loaf, I had decided, was destined for greater things and would live on in perpetuity. That evening after all guests had left for home, I carried the bread down to the basement where I got out my power drill and went to work.

By the end of the following day, my masterpiece was finished. I had drilled down through the center of the top crust and out the back to accommodate a metal rod, a power cord, a socket, a switch—all the components needed in order to turn the inedible loaf into a stylish lamp. A beautiful lampshade completed the effect, and it was now ready to return to Alison as a reminder of the day she tried to impress her boyfriend by creating a loaf of pumpernickel that allowed him to show off his woodworking skills. I presented it accompanied by a note that read, "Alison, I figured out how to make your bread a little bit lighter."

Once in a while something we've done, made, or created goes horribly wrong. But once in a while what might ordinarily be judged as a failure lives on as something even better than intended. I was sitting in the driver's seat having just pulled into the parking lot at the Massachusetts College of Art where I spent four years learning the skills that would hopefully propel me to a glorious career. I turned toward the back seat and carefully lifted the canvas that I had stretched tight over a wooden frame. It was an abstract oil painting, still wet with freshly-applied pigment, and the morning light coming through the windshield made the swirly designs and texture appear even more vivid.

As I slowly opened the driver's side door and shifted my position to step out with my masterpiece, a corner of the canvas caught the edge of the seat, and the painting fell face down onto the gritty pavement. It landed with a wet splat that sounded as if I'd emptied a bucket of wet seaweed and red Jello onto the sidewalk. (Don't ask me why red. Childhood food fights taught me that food always sounds sloppiest when it's the color of guts.)

My first impulse was to look around to see if any of my fellow classmates had seen my clumsy exit and the resulting debacle. With no one in sight, I proceeded to carefully lift one corner of the canvas to inspect the damage. It would be too late to amend whatever defacement had occurred, as the assignment was due that same day. Mr. Brant was unforgivingly strict about deadlines.

I lifted the piece gently using only two fingers, so as not to get wet paint on my hands. In so doing, the painting again fell face down onto the dirty asphalt and in my rush to save it, I instead kicked the corner causing it to skid several inches over the ground. Resigned to accept the inevitably tragic consequences, I flipped the piece over to inspect the damage.

Newly formed gouges in the wet paint had filled with rubble from the ground. Sand, small twigs, dried leaves, and unidentified debris had impregnated itself irreparably onto my masterpiece, leaving ugly gashes of litter in its wake.

With no possible options, I gently lifted the piece from the ground, took a deep breath, and embarrassingly presented it two hours later in front of the class, prepared to explain the artistic wreckage with a litany of lame excuses. Surprisingly, Mr. Brant spent a great deal of time critiquing my abstract painting, and commenting on the dramatic textures and unrestrained use of add-ins. I got an A-minus.

Sometimes, failed attempts lead to very consequential discoveries and life-changing inventions. Decades ago in the laboratories of the 3M Company, a scientist was researching strong adhesives and hoping to discover one that was even stronger than what already existed. What he found instead, however, failed miserably. His research had formulated an adhesive that bonded so lightly to surfaces that he thought it almost worthless. That is, until another of his colleagues at 3M took the adhesive and invented the Post-it note.

In the late 1800s an American inventor named Thomas Adams also ended up with a failed attempt to turn a substance called chicle into rubber. After repeated tries, his failed attempts eventually became what we now know as chewing gum.

Yet another scientist working at the DuPont Company in 1938 was hoping to create a new variety of chlorofluorocarbons for use as a refrigerant. When he came back to check his experiment, he was surprised to see that the gas in the refrigeration chamber had vanished, leaving only a few flakes of white material. Frustrated at the glaring failure of his experiment, he began to play with the strange residue and noticed it had a high tolerance for heat and had a low surface friction. We now make use of his failed experiment every time we cook in a pan coated with Teflon.

Not all failed attempts rise to the level of earth-shattering consequence. But even those failures that result in nothing more than a rock-hard loaf of bread sometimes become a stepping stone to go beyond failure and explore unexpected possibilities. Sometimes a failure is only temporary. Sometimes a failure is just a detour on the way to something even better. And sometimes it's just an excuse to have a good laugh.

So when life gives you lemons, make lemonade.

Or chewing gum.

Anti-Aging

It doesn't seem that long ago that I was in high school. Those days of playing practical jokes on my fellow classmates and struggling over homework are still fresh in my memory. I vividly recall counting down the days until summer vacation. First as a freshman, then a sophomore, a junior, and finally a senior. Now, I suddenly find myself a senior again. This time, I'm counting down the days until... well, let's not go there.

I can't say it came over me all of a sudden. But every once in a while I'm reminded that apparently there are adults walking around who are decades younger than myself. I know it seems strange to admit that I could be so unaware of my advancing years, but the jarring reality occasionally hits me when I least expect it.

The other day I was heading into the coffee shop when a young lady in front of me unexpectedly stepped aside to hold the door open for me. I appreciated the kind gesture and I, of course, thanked her. But, c'mon! Just because I have white hair doesn't mean I'm old. Or maybe she just wanted to get a better look at me from behind.

The signs keep showing up though. By now, I'm used

to getting senior discounts on things like movie tickets and bus fares. But still, my initial reaction is always, "Ha! I fooled them again." Then I remember that I'm the one who's the fool for not remembering how old I am. To date, however, no one has ever asked for my ID to prove my age. I've never been "carded" for a senior discount. Is it that obvious?

Although I may be in denial about my age, I sometimes do find myself repeating things. I even repeat things sometimes.

There are always reminders though. Something will cause me to recall a memory from an earlier era. It might be a movie with scenes from the 1950s, and I'll think *"That looks familiar."* Or it might be an event like the recent fiftieth anniversary of the first man on the moon that causes me to wonder, *"Has it been that long already?"* It doesn't seem that long ago that I watched the live broadcast on a black and white TV with my family. It might be something as simple as an old song from my high school days that causes me to reminisce. These outdated phenomena become jarring indicators of the endless procession of passing years. When I was a kid, for example, Coca-Cola cost a nickel and no one locked the doors of their house. Sometimes it's just a photograph of something that takes me back to my younger days when I was... well... *young*. A picture of a car with whitewall tires and a hood ornament. A service station attendant wearing a necktie and pumping gas for a customer. An old milk truck or the Good Humor man peddling ice cream from his musical truck.

Occasionally, I'll go into an antique shop where items I grew up with are on display as if they were dinosaur fossils. Dial telephones, slide rules, and typewriters are among the outdated things set out for sale at twice what they would have cost new. I'm still not yet willing to label these as antiques, because that would mean that I'm also getting older, which of course, I'm not. I do, however, reluctantly recall things from my youth that are, indeed from another era.

I remember the 24-volume set of books in my parents' living room called The Encyclopedia Britannica—a cumbersome and weighty collection so formidable that it came with its own bookcase. Although I have no recollection of ever having opened them, I found that several volumes stacked on top of one another provided a excellent platform on which to stand sufficiently high enough to reach the cookies in the kitchen cabinet. Volumes "A" through "E" usually did the trick. As I got older, "A" through "D" allowed me to get high enough. Then "A" through "C" and so on. By the time I was down to needing the support of just the "A" volume, I figured I had mastered everything the gigantic set had to offer. At that point, I put them away for good and thought, *"If there's something I need to learn, I'll just wait for someone to invent the Internet."*

Once in a while I'll hear something on the news that causes me to reassess time. I remember how shocked I was to hear that Kirk Douglas had died. Shocked, not that he died, but shocked that he had been still alive. And when my fifty-year high school reunion rolled around I was taken aback to see that many former classmates had apparently invited their parents to attend. I finally realized with some embarrassment that I was looking at simply older versions of... Oh, wait... is that *you*, Steve?

This led me to realize that aging is more easily observed

in other people. Looking in the mirror every day, the change I see in myself is so gradual, that it doesn't register. Or maybe it's just that my eyesight is getting worse. The wrinkles on my face (that is, if I had any) would be softened in a pleasing, out-of-focus blur that belies any signs of aging, were that ever to occur.

The supermarket where I sometimes shop has a "seniors only" hour each morning from eight to nine o'clock. As I walk the aisles I half expect some old person to stop me and say, "Hey! No young people are allowed in here until nine." So far, no one has approached me, but I attribute this to the fact that old people are just more polite, and don't want to make a scene. When I get old I'll remember to be polite too. Come to think of it, no store employee has ever stopped me from entering during senior hour for that matter, or asked to see my driver's license. Everyone there is just so polite.

Another "benefit" I've been privy to has been my AARP membership. The American Association of Retired Persons is an organization established for the benefit of older individuals with savings on everything from dining out to car insurance. It's intended for old people, but, somehow, I was able to sneak in the back door without being noticed. This unlikely participation has placed me on the receiving end of a constant barrage of junk mail. Every week I get at least two or three promotions for hearing aids and reduced rate prescriptions. Many of these promotions offer free merchandise such as duffel bags with the AARP logo stenciled on it. Even if I were to take advantage of any offers, I would decline the free gift. I wouldn't want to be seen walking around with an AARP duffel bag. Although, I guess I could tell people I got it from my Dad.

There are some things that certainly have changed during the few short years I've graced this planet. I don't deny that some are very different from the way I remember them. It wasn't that long ago when TV shows ran only in black and white, and newsmen who broadcast the latest headlines were often smoking cigarettes as they did so. The farthest you could walk with a telephone was the length of its cord. Printed pages were created one at a time on manual typewriters, and if you wanted additional copies, smelly, purple-inked duplicates called mimeographs was the tedious process by which you created them. Cars didn't have seatbelts, tattoos were for guys who had been in the Navy, and gay meant happy.

My wife tells me that my habitual patterns of behavior are signs that I might be aging. Granted, I have my one cup of coffee every morning like clockwork with no variation. The crew at the coffee shop doesn't even ask what I want. My large dark roast with half and half is handed to me as soon as I walk up to the counter. My weekly book group starts every Monday evening at seven o'clock on the dot, and the fact that you could set your watch by my predictable bedtime, she says, are all indications that I'm not immune to aging.

Some might call that being in a rut. But I like to think I'm in a groove.

No Hablo Español

It was late at night as we sat in the Atlanta airport awaiting our flight for the final leg of our trip home. We were returning from a medical mission to Honduras, where in the course of nine days, we had seen a total of twenty-eight hundred patients. Each day of our trip had brought us to a different remote village by way of dusty, rutted roads that snaked their way to obscure and desolate locations. I use the word "roads" warily. Much of the time, we were hanging on for dear life in the back of open pickup trucks bouncing over rocks and foraging our way through dense jungle.

In places, the ruts were filled with mud so deep that we'd have to get a running start and pray. Occasionally, the road would end at the edge of a river and we'd be forced to perilously drive into moving water that rose well up onto the truck doors. When one of our vehicles became hopelessly stranded in the middle of a deep stream we were forced to wade ashore and wait for it to be towed out.

Our procession of trucks usually numbered about three or four. The place to be, I quickly learned, was in the lead vehicle where there were no clouds of dust being kicked up by those in front of you. After sweating in near one hundred degree heat, by the time we reached our destination, people in the trucks at the rear looked like breaded veal cutlets.

Upon arriving at each village, despite there being only a handful of small shacks, we were typically greeted by hundreds of villagers patiently lined up under umbrellas shielding themselves from the hot sun. When villagers heard that the doctors would be arriving on a certain day, word spread quickly and the turnout of potential patients was overwhelming. Many villagers walked for miles while some arrived on horseback. At times, they seemed to materialize from nowhere out of the dense forest.

Hundreds of patients await our arrival in each village.

Okay, before we go any further let me just say, I'm not a doctor. Although I have been a patient at various times in my life, I have absolutely no medical training. Our team consisted of approximately five doctors, five nurses, a handful of medical students, and me. I was recruited by my friend Jack, a Physicians' Assistant, who has been leading these medical missions all over the world for years. He had assured me that if I ever wanted to accompany him on a trip, there would be plenty of tasks to be performed by someone who doesn't know the difference between a belly button and a lobotomy.

On this, my first trip, I had helped with crowd control, making sure lines of people were orderly. I also helped by setting up the pharmacy which consisted of ten huge suitcases filled with various medicines. Each day I'd find a shady out-of-the-way spot where I could arrange the medicines alphabetically for easy access. Although my Spanish vocabulary is limited to a very few words—*Hello, Yes, No, Please* and *Thank you*—I managed to not look like a complete idiot by using hand gestures and smiling a lot.

Now, as we sat awaiting our flight home, Jack regaled me with accounts from various medical trips he'd previously taken. One such trip to Africa was still fresh in his mind.

"You know, David, I just returned from Madagascar where I saw a one-man puppet show about tooth brushing performed in front of a huge audience of kids and adults."

I nodded my head as if to be enthralled.

"You know what a problem dental health is in Honduras don't you?"

Having seen firsthand the poor teeth of kids in Honduras, I again nodded, this time in agreement with his statement.

"You can talk to people about the importance of good dental hygiene," he continued, "but somehow the message doesn't always get through."

Now, because of the late hour, I wasn't sure if I was still

nodding, or just nodding off.

Jack continued. "But when this puppet show was being performed in the village, everyone was really paying attention. I know the message got through."

Then, he straightened his posture and asked me a question so out of the blue, that I wasn't sure I had heard it correctly.

"Would you be willing to do a puppet show on tooth brushing next year in Honduras?"

A puzzled look came over me as I stared at him. "You mean like in Spanish?"

"Well, of course," he replied in all seriousness.

"Doc, I don't speak a word of Spanish. And besides, I've never done a puppet show in my life."

Without fully thinking it through, I immediately added, "Alright, I'll do it."

Fast forward one year. After having bitten off more than I could chew, I was once again heading off to Honduras. This time, however, I carried with me a cast of characters in the form of professional puppets. The main character, a camel puppet whom I had dubbed "Señor Camello," was approximately two feet tall with a huge mouth that opened to reveal beautiful, white teeth. Other support cast members included a nurse puppet in uniform and a cute dog puppet. A collection of miscellaneous props would round out the show.

Still, having no experience with the Spanish language, I had written a four-page script for my show and had asked a friend to translate it. For the past three months I had been committing the translated script to memory by phonetically practicing what I had been told was the correct pronunciation.

Everywhere I went I could be seen silently mouthing the foreign words, memorizing one sentence at a time until finally I felt confident enough to do live performances in front of Spanish-speaking audiences while referring to my printed script only occasionally.

Now it was show time. Each day, I performed the one-man puppet show in a different remote village. Each day, crowds of people gathered to watch me instruct Señor Camello in proper tooth brushing techniques and its importance to overall health. I invited children to come up and take turns brushing the camel's huge teeth. At first they were shy, but as one stepped forward, others seemed happy to follow suit and take part in the performance. At the end of each show, people would line up as my puppets passed out hundreds of toothbrushes and tubes of toothpaste which had been donated by various dental companies back in the States.

Despite having performed this show now for several years to thousands of onlookers, my Spanish still has a long way to go. Each year, I begin phonetically memorizing my script a month or two before heading off to Central America. Each year I think to myself, *"This is the year I'm going to learn to speak Spanish."* And each year it doesn't happen. Oh, I've picked up a few words here and there simply by being among the beautiful citizens of Honduras. But as far as taking a foreign language course goes, it's something that still has not happened. For the time being, I'll have to rely on the few words I pick up during my annual visits.

But now, I'll have to wrap this up and end it here. I have to go to the baños. See? I'm learning already!

Just a Suggestion

When the ad agency I worked for in Boston decided to reduce office expenses, a suggestion box was prominently placed in the employee lounge. A sign directly above the box announced a fifty-dollar prize to be awarded each month for the best money-saving suggestion. At the end of the first month as the entries were read aloud by the office manager to the employees gathered in the lounge, one suggestion rose above all others as the undisputed winner.

As I stepped forward amidst scattered applause to accept my reward, the office manager shook my hand and re-read my simple money-saving suggestion—that the monthly prize should be reduced to twenty-five dollars. I thanked him and made sure he realized that the reduced award was to go into effect immediately after I had accepted my fifty dollar prize.

Occasionally I'd drop other suggestions into the box, but was never able to duplicate my initial success. Reducing the General Manager's salary was definitely not met with enthusiasm, since it was the General Manager who evaluated the suggestions. And apparently, my tongue-in-cheek suggestion of having the company artists use both sides of the tracing paper when doing layouts he did not think was even funny.

From time to time I think about something that, if I knew the right person to tell, I'd give them what I consider to be a brilliant suggestion. For example, I just don't know who to tell about my suggestion for an "OOPS" button on your computer or phone. "OOPS," or "Omit Opinions Previously Sent," would be for those occasional times when you realize the split second after you hit "send" that you inadvertently either sent your message to the wrong person, or you meant to say "sad you're not feeling well" instead of "glad you're not feeling well." Regardless of whether or not this suggestion might prove feasible, the CEO of Apple has never returned my calls.

Not all suggestions rise to a high level of importance. When the waiter comes to your table after your fancy French meal and suggests the creme broulée for dessert, no one cares if you go next door and get an Oreo cookie sundae with candy sprinkles instead. His offer was just a suggestion. And when you buy a frozen entree at the supermarket thinking that your meal will look like the picture on the package, read the fine print next to the photo. The words "serving suggestion" means that unless you hire a high-priced food stylist to prepare your meal for the camera, what you end up with may look more like a warmed up pile of scraps that you scraped up from the back seat of your car. Alternatively, you could just zap it in the microwave and close your eyes while you eat.

And I've never understood why the makers of certain health and medical products feel compelled to print some of the so-called "suggestions" on the labeling of their packages. Either they think people are stupid, or their company lawyers are trying to cover their ass. Either way, I guess this is why the needless instructions on my jar of dry skin cream say *"Suggested use: Apply liberally to dry skin."* Thank God I read that before I drank it.

Suggestions are just that. They're not mandates. No one expects every suggestion to be immediately adopted. Unless it's your wife who's suggesting it. When she suggests you clean the basement, it's more than a suggestion. Take my word for it. Turn off the TV and get busy.

Do you ever get annoyed when boarding a plane to see that the aisle is usually clogged with people trying to cram suitcases into overhead bins? My seat is inevitably beyond those blocking the aisle. Here's a suggestion for airlines: Allow passengers to board in any order they want. With one stipulation. Every passenger must proceed as far back in the aisle as possible and take the farthest available seat. That way, no one is trying to squeeze past them to get to a seat farther back in the plane. When you reach a point in the aisle where the boarding passengers in front of you block your progress, that's as far as you go. Take your seat and enjoy the flight.

And a suggestion for automobile companies... Ashtrays in cars should be optional equipment that cost extra. Why should I have to pay for someone else's smoking habit? Keep the cigarette lighters though. They come in handy when charging my phone.

Sometimes suggestions are tiny little things that might seem meaningless when seen on an individual scale, but when added together, can make a big difference. The shop where I get my coffee each morning provides wooden stir sticks so customers who add cream and sugar can mix it into their coffee. It's estimated that hundreds of acres of forest are leveled each year just to provide the wood necessary to make these disposable implements that are thrown away after three seconds of use. What if, instead of adding cream to your coffee, you put the cream into the cup first, then add the coffee to the cream. Voila! You no longer have to stir. The coffee itself does the mixing as it's poured in. It may seem a small, insignificant practice, but if enough of us get into the habit, it could make a difference. I practice this simple routine every day hoping the customers in line behind me will notice. But hey, it's just a suggestion.

The government could also use some suggestions. Not that I'm an expert at running a country, but if the work schedule of congressmen and senators did not include over 200 days off each year, maybe they'd actually get something done.

Not all suggestions are readily embraced. And for good reason. Years after my award-winning suggestion to reduce the cash prize for the best money-saving idea, I was partnered with a copywriter named Matt to come up with creative ideas as the ad agency we worked for was about to pitch the business of a company that made women's wigs and toupees for men.

"I have a suggestion," I boldly told him as we concluded one of our brainstorming sessions. "How 'bout we shave our heads for the presentation? We both walk in completely bald."

Matt raised his eyebrows skeptically and laughed right in my face. "That's the dumbest idea I've ever heard! I hope you're joking."

"It'll show them we're serious," I persisted. "I'll do it if you will. How 'bout it?"

Matt held up both palms in my direction. "Absolutely not! That's even worse than your suggestion to make business meetings more fun by replacing the conference room table and chairs with lawn furniture."

"But..." I began.

"No way in hell!" he interrupted. "Don't even think about it! I would never do anything that stupid."

Matt, grumbling under his breath, briskly headed back toward his office still shaking his head. At the last minute he turned to see me still standing in the corridor. "This discussion is over!" he barked before disappearing into his office.

"Okay," I said to myself as I heard the door slam behind him. "I'll take that as a maybe."

Unthinkable

Try not to think. Not only is that something most people would say is impossible, but it goes against everything we've been taught. Everything we learn from infancy requires thinking. Whether we're learning how to walk, talk, or use the potty, we are required to think. Even when we're not learning we're thinking. Every time we cross the street, put on our shoes, or see a pile of dog poop we're about to step in, we're thinking. Everything we see, hear, taste, smell, and touch automatically engages the human function known as thought.

As an adult, unless we're in an unlikely coma, we're constantly thinking. We think about what we're going to do today. We think about what we did yesterday. Even the most mundane and seemingly thoughtless acts require that we think. Opening a door, chewing our food, watching TV, and even scratching an itch all require thinking. Whether we're in a relaxed and leisurely state, or highly attentive, our brain communicates to us the identity of everything we observe during every second of every day. It all requires this involuntary brain function that is constantly active.

When I was in elementary school, my teacher, Mrs.

Betts, spent a great deal of her time trying to get us to think. If no one in the class appeared to know the answer to the question she had just asked, she'd stand firmly at the front of the classroom demanding that we think.

"Think" she'd insist to the class of nervous fifth-graders. Hands on hips, she'd repeat her command over and over with a look that demanded obedience. *"Think!"* It was her favorite word, although it was also an imperative the entire class often found difficult with which to comply.

"Boys and girls, think!" For some reason, she thought repetition of the word would somehow compel us to oblige. She somehow believed that by repeating the word, *"think,"* a flurry of intense brain activity would result in hands being raised by every student impatiently begging to be called upon for the correct answer.

It wasn't that we weren't thinking. We were all thinking. But what we were thinking about was usually not the answer to her question. We were usually not pondering the use of common denominators or the difference between verbs and adverbs. After several insistent commands to *"think,"* our adolescent brains were focused more on which student she would pick on to be the scapegoat, or how the scowl on her face made her wrinkles show up more, or how much her gray hair looked like a dirty floor mop. Sometimes, I confess, I was watching the clock and thinking about recess. I often found myself thinking, *"If one of my classmates would just think and give the right answer, we could stop thinking and get out of here."*

If Mrs. Betts, knew that after all the time she'd spent trying to get us to think, that decades later I'd be paying money to learn how to *not* think, she'd roll over in her grave. Rolling over, however, would require thinking. She's probably not doing much of that these days having died back in 1980 at the age of eighty-one.

The activity responsible for my unlikely affront to her teachings is something known as Transcendental Meditation. "TM" as it's called, is a specific form of meditation designed to create a peaceful state of mind resulting in lower blood pressure, calm awareness, and better overall health.

While all meditation shares this same ultimate goal, some forms of meditation are based on concentrated thought requiring focus on a specific point such as the breath, or the sound of a gong. Even this deliberate focus, however, requires thinking. Unlike these forms of meditation, TM is based on the principle of clearing one's mind of all thought. Sorry, Mrs. Betts, but that means no thinking. No focusing on your breath. No focusing on a sound. No focusing on anything. Attaining that state, however, is easier said than done.

That's where Transcendental Meditation comes in. TM was founded by Maharishi Mahesh Yogi who, in the 1960s, introduced the practice to people all over the world, including celebrities such as The Beatles. My instructor, Doctor Hart, received his training and certification in India and was now passing on his valuable knowledge to me by teaching me how to not think. Because TM requires one-on-one individual instruction by a trained facilitator, I sat alone with Doctor Hart at the Center for Peace and Wellness in Ipswich, Massachusetts. It was now twenty years since the practice had been introduced to the western world, and its popularity was still growing.

After several ritualistic ceremonies and offerings, my instructor taught me very specific techniques to clear my mind. This is the part Mrs. Betts wouldn't understand. That state of deep relaxation and peace is ultimately reached by clearing one's mind of all thought. In other words, by not thinking. No thinking about where you are. No thinking about any stimulus that might otherwise enter your field of awareness.

Because any visual image the eyes register causes brain activity resulting in thought, closing one's eyes is the first step in the process. Once in a comfortable bodily position, all tension held in the muscles dissipates. I was then given a specific mantra, unique to myself, that I was to share with no one. I was to silently repeat my mantra over and over in my mind.

Now, I know what you're thinking. This repetition, of course, must involve thought. And you'd be right. During this process, however, eventually even the thought of my mantra somehow magically disappears. If I notice a stray thought, no matter how small, enter my mind, I was to simply begin my mantra until, once again, my mind was cleared of all thought. Eventually, the need for this procedure would cease as there would be no conscious awareness of anything.

Studies have shown that those who practice TM for twenty minutes twice a day, benefit from a state of peace and improved health. I confess to not meditating as much as I should. Over the years, my dedication to not thinking has sometimes given way to an overabundance of thinking. It's a practice that takes... well... practice. Depending on how much mind chatter you have going on, persistent thoughts keep bubbling up. Sometimes these are thoughts about important life events and challenges, but other times the most insignificant thoughts arise from out of the blue. It might be the sound of a car driving by the house or a gust of wind outside. Sometimes it's the rustling of fabric as you move your leg just the tiniest bit.

Random thoughts from nowhere take turns interrupting my gradual, but intermittent journey to a total state of nothingness. Just when I'm almost there, another stray thought appears. This time it's the sensation of my arm resting on the chair, and I'm suddenly aware of where I am. I reposition it and return to my mantra as I attempt to sink into oblivion. As I clear my mind of all clutter, thoughts pass through with nowhere else to go but into my awareness. Another one bubbles up. It's the faint sound of the refrigerator motor turning on. This causes me to become abruptly aware that I'm meditating. The thought of Mrs. Betts suddenly enters my mind and I picture her, with hands on hips, trying to snap me out of this blasphemous activity by demanding that I think. In an ironic reversal of authority, I'm able to quickly dismiss her and return to my mantra.

Another minute passes and I become aware of yet another thought. This one's about a character I saw in a TV show a week ago. Where did *that* come from? And why now?

Back to my mantra. Several more seconds pass. I'm sinking deeper and deeper into that blissful state of being. I have lost almost all sense of awareness. Deeper... Deeper.......

My stomach gurgles. Back to reality. I'm momentarily reminded that I'm in a body sitting here in my living room. But the distraction is brief. I'm able to put it out of my mind almost immediately.

Until... F i . . .

n a l . . .

l y . . . . .

The Fuck-it List

We all have things we'd like to do, places we'd like to go, and goals we'd like to achieve at some point in our lives. These life-long dreams on our "bucket list" are the things we hope to accomplish before we ourselves kick the proverbial bucket. Some things on our bucket list might be seen as quite achievable, but we just haven't gotten around to making them happen. Things like attending a Broadway play, planting a vegetable garden, taking an RV trip across the country, learning a new language, or taking up square dancing.

Other bucket list items might be viewed quite correctly as improbable. While we may wonder what it would be like to skydive, run a marathon, or climb Mount Everest, the chances of realizing these goals may, for most of us, be far from a realistic goal.

Some bucket list items we put off for no other reason than we just can't seem to make time for them. Others we push into the ever-extending future because of financial constraints. For me, I've never been to Italy, so that's something that's not only on my list, but certainly within the realm of possibility. I'd also like to learn Spanish, and while this pales in comparison to climbing Everest, I have only myself to blame for not making the time to do so.

Decades ago, a friend of mine made it known to all of us that if the opportunity ever presented itself, he would jump at the chance to be launched into space in a rocket ship. Gary talked about it every chance he got, and we all knew it was the primary item on his bucket list. If the opportunity ever really came up, however, we all knew he'd make up some lame excuse to back out. "Oh, I'd love to, but I have a haircut this afternoon."

Another of my friends, Carl, held out the most unlikely hope that he would one day go on a date with Jennifer Lopez. While I would put both of these possibilities in the "next to impossible" column, I would consider it more likely that I would sooner see Gary's scrawny figure walking around on the moon than I would Carl walking anywhere in the vicinity of Jennifer Lopez.

Far be it from me, however, to judge someone else's hopes and dreams. Everyone has a different bucket list and different reasons for wanting those things to become a reality. We all need goals no matter how unlikely they might seem. If we had no hopes and dreams, nothing to aspire to, our lives would be boring with few exciting possibilities to look forward to. If becoming a multi-billionaire had been on the bucket list of teenager Bill Gates, I'm sure even he would have thought it extremely remote at best. And had Barack Obama not dared to dream impossible dreams, he might be taking your order at Burger King.

The older I get, however, the more unlikely some items on my bucket list seem to become. Now that I'm in my seventies, I doubt if I'll ever climb Mount Everest. I also see my hopes of becoming a pitcher for the Boston Red Sox becoming more remote with every day that passes. It's these unlikely items that, while it would have been nice to see them realized, have now become impossible. So rather than continue to hold on to these former dreams as possibilities, I have given up hoping that they might yet be achieved. They still hold a fascination for me, but I have now seen the reality of the situation. They are never going to happen. So I have transferred them to my "Fuck-it List."

This designation, however, does not mean that I don't think about them. It does not stop me from daydreaming about these experiences. It simply means that my daydreams are as far as they'll ever go. I still enjoy thinking about them and wondering what the actual experiences would have been like had I been fortunate enough to live them. I still wonder how I would have fared if given the opportunity to scuba dive with sharks or race in the Indianapolis 500. Thanks to my vivid imagination, these daydreams sometimes have a surprising degree of reality as I imagine myself actually experiencing some of those things. In my last Red Sox game, for example, I pitched a shutout against the Yankees.

It may not be quite as satisfying as having actually lived these dreams, but I still enjoy imagining them. There's also a plus side to living the experience only in my mind. I get to enjoy the positive aspects with none of the drawbacks or negative side effects that go along with some of these extreme adventures. I never get eaten by a shark, and after I climb to the top of Mount Everest, I can just sit back down on the sofa and watch TV. Fuck it!

Make No Sudden Movements

It was kind of a ritual with us. Nearly every Tuesday evening, my parents and I found ourselves at the 3G's Restaurant in Georgetown, Massachusetts seated at our usual table. It wasn't the food that kept us coming back week after week, although the casual Italian fare was certainly adequate. The 3G's featured a much more unusual offering that made the twenty-minute drive well worth the trip, and an outing we looked forward to with great anticipation.

Having scanned our menus, we were now ready to order our meal. Getting the attention of our waitress, however, was always a delicate endeavor and one that, if not done carefully, could end up costing you a lot of money. It had nothing to do with the disposition or attitude of our server. She was not about to rush up to our table and bash our sculls in with a pepper mill if we seemed too demanding. She was not going to double the price of our pasta if we appeared too anxious to get her attention. Marion was a friendly waitress, and one we'd come to know by name from our many previous visits. She would never have done anything to inflict injuries on us or even make us feel bad if we were to impatiently summon her.

But raising your hand in the air would be a gesture you might come to regret. Even the slightest nod of your head could become an unintended action for which you'd later find yourself paying dearly.

This was a restaurant in which you had to be very subtle with your movements. We learned to talk without using hand gestures. The request of "pass the ketchup please" was issued without pointing at the bottle. Even the raising of a wine glass in a simple toast was an action that could be accompanied by a serious and expensive consequence.

This was not the result of a strict management policy initiated by some overly-sensitive but paralyzed restaurant manager who viewed every such bodily movement as mocking his lack of mobility. Nor were our carefully restricted movements due to guard dogs posted at the corners of the dining room trained to respond to any sudden or suspicious movement by unleashing a surprise attack.

There was, however, a man sitting at the front of the room whose job it was to keep a keen eye out for the slightest gestures of customers and to immediately respond accordingly. At his side stood a helper who also scanned the room looking for subtle movements of the diners to call to his attention.

George was an auctioneer. And amid the hubbub of customers enjoying their meals, he would search out the slightest hint of someone responding to his request for a higher bid. "Do I hear twenty-five dollars? Now thirty. Do I hear thirty? I have thirty. Now Forty." Usually, a subtle nod was all it took to acknowledge your acceptance of the current bid price. Once bidding on an item was underway, it often went rather quickly, and the frantic process could catch an unaware diner by surprise. This was not the time to summon your waitress by raising your hand.

It didn't take much to place a bid. You didn't have to frantically raise your hand like some first-grader hoping to be called on in class for the correct answer. A subtle nod or the slightest raising of one finger was all it took. Unless you wanted to become the proud owner of an antique porcelain bedpan, you learned to wait until George had yelled "sold" before asking for the dessert menu.

Tonight we were in no hurry to leave. We weren't going anywhere, and Marion would get to us in her own time. In the meantime, we waited for each auction item to be held up and described to the room of patrons. Shoved under our table were a few things on which we'd already successfully been high bidder—an old tea kettle, a pair of vintage opera glasses, a box of old clock parts, and a framed print of a half-naked maiden becoming disturbingly friendly with a sheep.

My mother and I each rented space in a group antique shop in nearby Newburyport, Massachusetts. It was a fun hobby that paid for itself and then some. But the most enjoyable aspect of this venture was what we considered the treasure hunt. Gathering collectibles and other items to sell was not only fun, but it taught us the value of various antiques and other items. If we could buy something for ten dollars and sell it for twenty, it made up for the things we bought that languished unsold in our shop for years.

The next item up for bids was a box of old kitchen utensils that George could not seem to even give away. When he lowered the opening bid to ten dollars still with no takers, he started dumping other items into the box—a couple of old books and a small figurine of a frog.

"Alright, who'll start this off at ten dollars?" His offer was met with deafening silence except for the sound of silverware clinking on plates. His runner brought additional items to throw into the box. A handful of vintage postcards, an old sewing kit, and a pair of candlesticks. Finally a few hands went up. The entire box of stuff finally went for about twenty-five dollars after George had added even more items. This was George's way of making sure he got rid of everything— filling boxes until something caught someone's eye. But the buyer had to take the whole box, and occasionally, multiple boxes. Someone who might have had their eye on a nice wind-up clock often had to lug home boxes of mismatched dishes and the odd lampshade.

George, who was probably in his early seventies at the time, often became the brunt of practical jokes perpetrated by his runner, Brian. As he brought various items to be auctioned to the front of the room for bidding, he would attempt to get George to crack a smile. Placing a decorative serving bowl upside down on George's head or wrapping a fancy lady's shawl multiple times around his neck was enough to cause good-natured laughter among the diners, but seldom broke George's serious concentration of getting bids on the items. Because of this unscheduled floor show, even people who came only for dinner enjoyed their evening, and often returned the following week for more antics at George's expense.

As you've no doubt gathered, the 3G's auction was by no means what one would consider upscale. This was not an exclusive Christie's or Sotheby's auction. There were no high-priced pieces of furniture or beautiful carpets, no expensive oil paintings and no fine antique gold and silver jewelry. This was more of a Honey-look-what-I-found-in-the-cabinet-under-the-kitchen-sink kind of affair. Oh, and with Lasagna.

As time passed and the hour became later, George began dumping more odds and ends into large boxes and practically giving them away. A tin beer tray was thrown in with an empty jewelry box. Then a ceramic piggy bank. Seeing some interest, he took advantage of the opportunity to get rid of some items that had been previously passed over. A Donald Duck hand puppet was added, then a kid's pail and shovel that looked like it had been run over by a car. Then a wooden cutting board in the shape of a whale. More and more things were added to the box until he was finally able to yell, "sold!"

By the time everything was finally sold, we had claimed our share of pieces we felt could be marked up in price enough to make it worth our while. A vintage ashtray with its own stand, a pair of marble bookends, a brass wall sconce, an old kerosene lamp that came with an entire box of broken and useless woodworking tools, and a stack of vintage comic books.

As patrons paid their dinner tabs and headed out the door to the parking lot, we gathered our purchases and, along with other successful bidders, went to turn in our bidding numbers and settle up at the auction desk. Marion had just finished clearing our table, and as we finally walked toward the exit we were able to turn and unabashedly wave goodbye without fear of having to pay extra for the gesture.

A Very Literal Take

I flew down the street on my skates as a few casual bystanders watched, waiting to see if I would fall. Having disappointed them, I slowed my speed to a controlled stop at the edge of an intersection. One of the observers, seeing that I was now standing still, approached me with a stern expression and pointed to a sign on a nearby pole.

"No Roller-blading," he shouted. "Can't you read?"

Sure enough, the man was correct. The message he was pointing to stood out in big, bold letters. "NO ROLLER-BLADING." I smiled and responded in the most polite voice I could muster in the moment, while in my mind, I was thinking *I hope this jerk's not doing this to impress his girlfriend.*

"Roller-blade is a brand name," I said. "These aren't Roller-blades. These are called Land-Rollers. So I'm not roller-blading!"·

I must confess that, having been aware of the presence of these signs, I've always secretly been prepared for this encounter. I had hoped, however, that it would be a police officer who would approach me so I could call to his attention this flawed and overly-specific law. I would never be discourteous to a police officer, however, and the scenario has played out only in my head. After the imagined encounter, he'd holster his revolver and we'd both laugh before I'd eventually skate away on my Land-Rollers.

I've always been very literal. Especially when it comes to the law. If there's any place where words should be taken literally, it's the law. Laws are not suggestions. They're rules to be taken at their word—Literally. Yet, it somehow always pleases me whenever I can find a loophole in a law. It's a silent game I play with myself. If I can spot the "law flaw," I win.

Hat's off (literally) to the motorcyclist who, back in the 1960s, found a loophole in the recently-enacted Massachusetts law requiring motorcycle riders to wear helmets. He was stopped by the state police when they spotted him riding with the wind blowing through the hair of his uncovered head. He pointed out that he, indeed, was wearing a helmet. He just happened to be wearing it on his knee. The law was quickly changed to be more specific.

Traffic laws have always been good candidates for discovering rules that have not been completely thought through. One of my pet peeves has always been motorists who barely slow down at stop signs. You've seen them. They believe stop signs are not to be taken literally, but merely as something to consider if it's convenient to do so. Now, don't get me wrong. There are times at an intersection when visibility is good and there are no other cars anywhere in sight when a complete stop is not really necessary. I'm occasionally guilty of taking liberties with the law at these times. But a driver who rolls right through a stop sign, barely slowing down at a busy intersection when I'm trying to cross the street is putting me and others in danger. I've imagined myself calling his attention to the violation by pulling the offender from his car and punching him repeatedly in the face. When he complains and yells at me to stop punching him, I imagine myself cleverly asking, "Do you want me to stop? Or should I just slow down?"

One place in which literal ambiguity is used to advantage is advertising. TV commercials have always been very adept at hedging their language in order to imply something without literally saying it, and I always have fun trying to spot the offending ad. One ambiguous phrase I've noticed are the words "up to." To most viewers of a TV commercial these words don't even register, yet this simple phrase has enormous meaning.

"Save up to fifty percent," for example, has almost no meaningful promise of savings, although most viewers hearing this believe they are about to save fifty percent. But listen closely and take the words literally. "Up to" literally means "less than" or "not more than." That means any amount less than fifty percent is a valid fulfillment of their misleading claim. One percent is less than fifty percent, and therefore meets the requirements of their pitiful offer.

"Lose up to fifty pounds guaranteed" is another claim we've all heard on weight loss commercials. Taken literally, this so-called claim promises nothing more than the fact that any amount of weight loss less than fifty pounds is all it takes to fulfill their meaningless promise.

Some advertising even uses the word "literally" thinking it somehow legitimizes what they're saying. It doesn't. It simply makes it clear they've not really thought about their words. I heard a TV commercial the other night about switching your cell phone service. According to the announcer, signing up for their service is "literally the best decision you'll ever make." While their service might be less costly than some, and signing up for it might be a good idea, I daresay, deciding not to step out into the street in front of that bus qualifies as a slightly better decision than switching your cell phone service, thus making their absurd claim literally untrue.

But signage and advertising are by no means the only flagrant violators of literal correctness. People literally misuse the word "literally" all the time in speech. See? I just did. What I should have said was that people literally misuse the word "literally" *some* of the time. But that's understandable. We can't hold people to such strict standards for offhanded remarks used in conversation.

"I'm literally starving" when someone hasn't eaten since breakfast, or "It's literally freezing in here" when the thermostat is set to only sixty degrees are examples where we should cut people some slack (not literally.) They're just trying to make a point. But when a message is committed to advertising or printed signage, someone had to have given it more than just a passing thought. They had to think about it and spend money to have it produced.

In recent years, discovering examples of wording, that when taken literally, exposes flawed logic, has for me, become almost a sport. I was recently looking for a place downtown to park my car and noticed a bank parking lot with several empty spaces. As I pulled into the lot, I was confronted by a sign that read "Parking for Bank Customers Only." I paused to think about what that literally meant.

"I'm a bank customer," I reasoned. Okay, maybe not a

customer of that particular bank. But it doesn't say that. I ultimately decided not to park there, but I gave myself points for discovering yet another instance where taking something literally changes the intended meaning.

Similarly, I was in a local store not long ago wandering around looking for a restroom. At the back of the store in the corner was a closed door behind which was what I assumed to be the object of my search. A sign on the door, however, read "Employees Only." Disappointed, I started to walk away thinking, if I hadn't been retired, I'd still be employed, and therefore, eligible to enter. Granted, I'd not have been an employee of that particular store. But the sign was not specific about where you had to be employed.

Alright, I know I'm being overly picky. And I know I'm occasionally guilty of the very violations I rail against. So if you happen to witness one of these extremely rare occasions in which I say something that I don't mean to be taken literally, don't get your feathers all ruffled and make a mountain out of a molehill. There's no sense in beating a dead horse over a simple slip of the tongue. So don't jump down my throat. Oops, there I go again.

When Saliva Turns to Spit

It was the second day of the workshop. About ten of us sat on pillows on the floor, eyes closed, in a semi-meditative state as the facilitator led the group through visualizations intended to increase our awareness of perception. After leading us deep into various sensory exercises, he instructed us to amass a large amount of saliva in our mouths. After a few minutes, quite certain that everyone had done so, he handed a paper cup to each of us. He then had us bring the cups to our mouths, deposit the accumulated saliva into the cup and set it down in front of us.

After only a minute or so, he had the group collect more saliva in our mouths, pick up our cups, and add to our initial deposit, once more setting the cups back down in front of us. After another moment of silent, but perplexed relaxation, we were yet again instructed to bring the cups to our mouths. This time, however, we were told to drink the entire contents of our cups. Even during what was intended to be a silent meditation, a disgusted chorus of groans could be heard. Keep in mind, this was our own saliva, still warm, having been in our mouths only a few moments before—the very same secretion that exists in our mouths every minute of every day. Nothing about it had changed.

The point at which saliva turns to spit is commonly thought to be at precisely the instant it leaves our mouths. In reality, the only thing that changes, however, is our perception of it. It has undergone no chemical change, no radical shift in its physical properties. But our perception adamantly suggests otherwise. And it is our perception to which we remain unfaltering slaves. There is no thought or event brought into our awareness that is not filtered through our perception. It is the only way we humans are capable of gathering information. The truth of what happens around us matters little. It is our *perception* of what happens around us to which we react, regardless of what may actually be happening.

If we see something that appears to be fearful, beautiful, or sad, it is because we have observed it and judged it as such. That then becomes our truth—our reality. It can be no other way. Different people may, in fact, see the same thing in quite different ways. This may be due to our history or past experiences. This may also change depending on how something is presented to us. At times, our perception may in fact be deliberately manipulated by others for a specific purpose.

Those who manipulate our perception know that the way in which we perceive something is totally changeable. They understand that our so-called "reality" is not absolute. It is flexible—putty in the hands of those who have a stake in how something appears to us.

This was brilliantly brought to light in one of my class assignments at the Massachusetts College of Art in Boston, where one of my required freshman classes was drawing. The course was taught by Mister Orr, a graduate of the same college, and still fairly young. The assignment, as it was presented, sounded simple enough. Each student was to choose a common, familiar object and draw a picture of it.

Hmm, I thought. *That sounds easy.* I'm sure all of my fellow classmates felt the same way. After all, we were still very full of ourselves having come right out of high school where we had all been the stand-out students of our respective art classes. I couldn't wait to show off the drawing skills that had propelled me to the top of my high school art class. Looking smugly around the room I felt certain my work would once again prove that my admission to the top art college in the country was not unfounded.

While I sat quietly anticipating the praise I would receive for my work, Mister Orr further added to the parameters of the assignment.

"The object you choose to draw," he explained, "cannot be something you see in this room. You must draw the object from memory."

Okay, I thought. *That still sounds simple enough.*

But Mister Orr was not done. "And whatever you choose to draw must not be drawn realistically. You are to draw the *personality* of the object. Decide how the object feels to you and depict that feeling in your drawing. Draw the *nature* of the object—its temperament if you will. Oh, and you have exactly one hour to complete your work."

With that, he left the room, leaving behind a class full of bewildered freshmen wondering what just happened. As we glanced around at the confused looks on each others' faces I realized that if I didn't quickly think of an object to draw I wouldn't have time to actually draw it.

A flower, I thought. *No, too predictable. A chair, no, a bicycle, an ice cream sundae.* Realizing I would have to assign a personality to whatever I chose to draw had me rethinking everything that came to mind.

I'm pretty good at drawing cars, I rationalized, *but what does the personality of a Buick look like?* After rejecting dozens of candidates, I finally settled on what I thought would lend itself to a perfect solution to Mister Orr's baffling assignment.

My drawing of a toilet was not only an adequate piece of art, but also a brilliantly clever take on assigning personality to such a mundane object. The squat, flabby contours of the object in my drawing reflected what I perceived to be the submissive character of this common, utilitarian fixture. Its vapid, self-effacing yawn willingly takes all the crap we give it, all while cowering passively beneath us. I eyed the chalky-white, bland image on the pad in front of me, satisfied that it uniquely captured the subservient personality inherent in the object itself. As Mister Orr re-entered the room I proudly grinned and prepared to accept the accolades for my superior art skills as well as my cleverly conceived solution to his assignment.

But Mister Orr was still not done. He astonished the class when he said that he did not want to see our drawings. He told us instead to rip our drawings to shreds and deposit them into the trash receptacle he had placed at the front of the room.

Okay, I thought to myself. *Now this is getting weird.*

One by one, we reluctantly trudged up, dropped our masterpieces into the trash and headed back to our easels to wait for an explanation. After the last of the students had made the slow round trip, Mister Orr stood to address the class. He explained that an artist should never become too attached to any piece of work.

Okay, point taken, I thought. *I get it.* Furthermore, my disappointment at having to shred my masterpiece only served to emphasize his premise. But it was the next half of the day's assignment that remains one of the most memorable lessons of my entire college career. I say "lesson" and not "assignment" because what our young instructor did next changed my understanding of perception. He surveyed the class with a smirk, knowing that what he was about to say would cause our young brains to implode.

"Ladies and gentlemen," he began, "think of the object you just drew and the personality you assigned to it. Now imagine what the opposite of that personality would be and draw the same object with that opposite character. I'll be back in half an hour."

With that, Mr. Orr again left the room leaving us behind to rethink the character of our original drawings. The pastel rendering I had just thrown into the trash perfectly personified the toilet as the wishy-washy, submissive fixture resigned to constantly seeing the worst side of us without complaint. Now I found myself attempting to redefine that very same object in a way contrary to my initial perception.

With little time to rethink, my first reaction was to set aside the milky-white pastels and bland, gray paper I had previously used to convey the toilet's personality. I removed a paintbrush and a bottle of black, India ink from my art box and opened my pad to a page of bright orange paper. I cleared my mind of all preconceptions and began without much thought.

Half an hour passed and my final drawing of what had now morphed into an angry and aggressive toilet was more than just a complete reversal of my initial depiction. It was more than the bold and jagged, black strokes portraying its large gaping mouth now snapping and ready to rip its owner to shreds. It was not just the drawing that had changed. My understanding of perception and an artist's ability to control it had been completely upended. I was learning that the way in which we perceive something is malleable and can be altered.

We are witness to this every day. Lawyers might try to alter our perception by the way in which they present a case. Politicians do it all the time in the way they position an argument, or cite misleading facts.

I don't mean to say that all of this is necessarily a bad thing. If we held staunchly to only our own preconceived ideas, we'd miss out on the effect of movies, music, art, and so much of what we find enjoyable. A lizard or salamander that might ordinarily give us the creeps, for example, is seen as a cute little spokesperson for an insurance company, and we think, *"How adorable!"* Or a furry little bear cub that looks warm and cuddly, when presented on a giant Cinematic screen accompanied by foreboding music, suddenly becomes a monster that scares the hell out of us.

It's that twist at the end of a story, the surprise ending to a film, the unexpected plot revelation that keeps us from replaying our own narrow-minded thought patterns. Even the punchlines of jokes are often effective only because they surprisingly upend our initial perceptions.

Whenever I sense that my perception has been changed,

I am reminded of Mister Orr's drawing class and the day he changed my perception of perception. And I am grateful that my mind is capable of being flexible. Without this ability to change how we perceive something we'd be limited to those closed-minded patterns that have been locked up in the cold storage of our separate minds. Life would indeed be a repetition of preconceived beliefs.

Perception, for all its false narratives and distorted views, is a valuable tool that we use to determine what's happening around us and how we should react to it.

Yes, for all its flaws, perception is a funny thing. At least that's the way I perceive it.

Goodnight Mr. Mayor

It was the middle of the night. 1965. I was a freshman in college and my buddies and I were excited to be visiting New York City. We were just returning from a night in Greenwich Village, epicenter at the time, of the burgeoning hippie scene. The four of us had made our way into one of the clubs and found ourselves in a dark cellar overwhelmed by smoke and loud music. Finding no place to sit, we inconspic- uously leaned against a back wall and tapped our feet to the strains of *"Do You Believe in Magic."*

After an hour or so, John Sebastian, later to become the singer/songwriter and leader of the famous group, The Lovin' Spoonful, had finished his set and passed a hat for donations. Declining his offer to part with a few dollars, we found our way back to the street and crammed ourselves into our vintage 1950 Dodge panel truck and headed uptown. We always enjoyed traveling to gigs in the dingy, red truck, although our joy was always tempered by the perpetual fear that some three-dollar engine part would finally give way to years of neglect and leave us stranded. Being a rock band ourselves, we had dreams of becoming so successful that one day we, too, might play at some smoky, underground club and pass our own hat.

I can't say we did not have some degree of our own success. We were constantly booked at fraternity house parties at colleges and Universities all over New England, and had taken it upon ourselves to book large venues on Cape Cod and various other popular places. We also had a regular weekly gig at The Rathskeller in Kenmore Square in Boston where students would materialize from all over the city to listen to live rock music and use their fake I.D.s to buy beer.

We had named our van "Lucille" in tribute to the well-known fact that legendary blues singer, B.B.King, had christened his guitar with the same name. Although the names were identical, the sounds coming from his famous musical instrument bore no resemblance to some of the hellish sounds frequently heard coming from the underside of our truck.

On the side of the van I had painted a nearly life-size cartoon mural of our band, complete with guitars, bass, and drums. In huge lettering above the cartoon figures was the name of our band, "The Luv Lace Lads." In addition to providing some free advertising, this also prevented people from mistaking us for a legitimate commercial enterprise such as a flooring company, a plumber, or an exterminator.

Traffic being what it was at 3 a.m., we arrived at our destination all the way up on 88th Street in a matter of minutes. Gracie Mansion was a historic landmark built in 1799, and for decades had served as the official residence of the Mayor of New York City. The Mayor at the time, was the Honorable Robert F. Wagner, who at this moment, was undoubtedly sound asleep.

As we rattled our conspicuous looking vehicle up to the guard shack, the two armed officers could tell instantly that we were not from a flooring company and became instantly suspicious.

"Excuse me, we're going to have to ask you to turn around and leave the premises immediately. This is private property. This is the Mayor's residence."

Our lead guitarist, Ken, who was behind the wheel of Lucille, now became more polite than we had ever seen him as he rolled down his window.

"Yes, Sir. We know. We're guests of the Mayor and he invited us to spend the night here."

The guard took a step back and looked to his companion as he moved his right hand slowly toward his holstered revolver.

"What's in the van?" he asked, now becoming visibly more aggressive.

At that moment the remaining three of us leaned forward toward the open driver's side window. "It's just us!" we all asserted in unison.

Both guards became startled at the sudden appearance of a group of long-haired hipsters, and in hindsight, it now seems probable that they expected us to leap from the van brandishing firearms. Of course, nothing could have been further from the truth, although had we been so equipped, I might have picked up my guitar and regaled them with a few bars of a Rolling Stones song to prove our point.

"We're a rock band from Massachusetts," Ken tried to explain. "The Mayor hired us to play at his party last night, and he invited us to spend the night here."

"Really!?" the guard asserted.

I couldn't tell if it was actually a question or a sarcastic comment, but it was clear he wanted more information. As Ken continued to explain, one of the guards retreated to the guard shack and picked up a loose-leaf binder.

"After we played our last set around midnight," Ken continued, "we decided to drive down to Greenwich Village and go to a club. We figured we'd be recognized when we returned, and they'd let us back in. But when we left here, there were different guards on duty."

Still suspicious, though now slightly less intimidating, the officer explained that there had, indeed, been a changing of the guard at 2 a.m.

"If you are in fact guests of the Mayor, your name would be on the list of the registry in the guard house."

The second guard, still scanning the pages of the binder, stopped at one entry, and called out to his partner, "Luv Lace Lads. Here it is. They're good."

Clearly surprised, the first guard softened his tone, told us where to park, and added that someone would meet us at the side door. He asked us to be as quiet as possible when entering the mansion. We had previously received such instructions from a member of the servant staff at the time we had left for our Greenwich Village outing, but Ken nodded as if we were hearing this for the first time. The second guard picked up a phone and called in to the night staff to announce our entry as we slowly proceeded, bringing Lucille to a quiet stop at a side entrance—as capable as she was, at any rate, of demonstrating "quiet."

A butler, or whoever he was, met us at the door with a

degree of politeness unexpected in the middle of the night. Leading us to a restaurant-size kitchen where, despite the staff having quit for the night, he explained that the Mayor had given us total access to anything we wanted in any of the several refrigerators in the room. He cracked open the door of one, noting that there were left-overs from the night's party.

"There are quite a few light snacks here. And if you're hungrier, there are still a couple of baked turkeys and a ham," he pointed out. "There are knives in the drawer to cut them up. Help yourselves."

Our eyes widened at the prospect, since we had not taken advantage of the vast array of party food while we were playing for the dignitaries and other guests. We had not been introduced to any of the well-dressed party-goers, so I can only assume, having been guests of the Mayor, that they were dignitaries of some sort, and not simply members of his bowling league.

The butler further explained that, while he was not permitted to provide us access to any liquor, there were soft drinks in yet another fridge. He then showed us up to the second floor where we each had our own bedroom. We had been told that we were to be out of Gracie Mansion by ten o'clock the following morning, but that the kitchen staff would be back early to prepare a nice breakfast for us.

I don't recall partaking of any of the food, as I was about to fall asleep standing up. Nor do I recall how we were fortunate enough to be hired to play at the Mayor's party. It was our manager, Bill, who scheduled our gigs. We simply went where we were told. And since we had been told to vacate the premises by the following morning, I went straight to bed.

Upon awakening after way too little sleep, we all shuffled down to the kitchen for breakfast, loaded up Lucille with our gear, and slowly made our way to the entrance gate. The same two guards who had allowed us entry were still on duty, and they unlocked the gate, waving us through. Had I thought at the time about the political ramifications of such an imprudent declaration, I like to think I would not have said what came out of my mouth as we drove past the guard shack.

"We're exterminators," I yelled from the back of the van. "Just making sure there are no more rats in the house."

The Monster in The Dungeon

Halfway down the creaky cellar staircase was as far as I dared venture unaccompanied. From there I could see, lurking in the unwelcome darkness, the huge coal-eating furnace waiting to devour little four-year-old kids like myself. Behind the ancient wooden staircase lay a mountain of filthy coal, deposited there by means of a small ground-level window, and shoveled regularly by one of my relatives into the fiery innards of the huge furnace. The rank and putrid coal dust irritated my young nostrils, adding to the treachery of what my cousin called the dungeon. I dared not descend any farther into the hellish underworld.

Built in 1880, the huge, fifteen-room house majestically dominated the corner of Cedar and Highland Streets in the Roxbury neighborhood of Boston. The matriarch of the household was my great-grandmother, Nanny, and over the decades, it had been, and still was, home to generations of extended family members. Aunts, uncles, and cousins as well as my grandmother and my great-grandmother still resided here. Relatives like my own mother had been born and also married within the confines of the grand home. Ancestors had died there. The house was clearly the remnant of a bygone era, although as a child, it was all I had known. For all its ghosts and mysterious, hidden rooms, it was full of laughter and love.

At its uppermost extremity, the farthest one could distance himself from the dreaded dungeon, was the attic, and my home for the first several years of my life. While this may conjure up images of a cramped and creepy bat-infested loft above a trap door at the top of a pull-down ladder, it was far from that. While no palace, the attic was comfortable enough for me and my parents to call home. Until my sister was born, it was home to just the three of us. We had a living room, a big bedroom, and plenty of storage. We even had our own kitchen, although even as a four-year-old, I had to squeeze past my mother if she happened to be at the stove. I fell asleep each night to the eclectic sounds of the city and was often awakened from my slumber by fire and police sirens screaming down Cedar Street. Occasionally, a ghoulish dream about the monster dwelling three flights down in the dungeon jolted me out of a sound sleep. For the most part, however, the attic felt friendly and cozy.

We were in no way, however, limited to these few modest rooms. Nanny's house was very much a communal living space. Downstairs from our attic hideaway was the second floor where lived my great-aunt, Nonnie. She and her husband along with their children also had their own kitchen. Living quarters were in no way, however, locked off or otherwise separated. No doors prevented others from walking wherever they wanted throughout the entire three-story structure and, in fact, was encouraged. We were all one huge family and many of the rooms were considered the domain of all who lived there.

The entire fifteen rooms, however, were accommodated by a single bathroom on the second floor. Despite this, I never remember having to wait in line for my turn, although now that I think about it, I was in diapers most of the time I lived there. Bath water was shared by relatives one after another on bath night, with the dirtiest going last. I regularly earned that distinction, as I recall being often allowed the thrilling duty of pulling the plug to allow the dirty water to gurgle down the drain.

102 Cedar Street, Roxbury, Mass., ca. 1940s

Downstairs on the ground floor was where my relatives spent much of their time. My great-grandmother's kitchen was a gathering place where aunts, uncles, and cousins along with my grandmother, my parents, and my great-grandmother herself could often be found. Every night after dinner, I'd intrude on the dinner tables of other relatives to see what they were having to eat. If I was lucky, I was sometimes able to procure and extra dessert. For Saturday supper, widely known in New England for beans, hot dogs, and brown bread, Nanny would make a big crock of baked beans and offer them to all household residents for a few cents a bowl. It became her specialty for decades.

The ground floor also featured a huge parlor that was reserved for Christmas and other celebrations such as my parents' wedding. Across the hall was another large room with a big upright piano from which strains of Beethoven and other classical composers would occasionally emanate. That's how you'd know that Alfie, another of my great-uncles, was in the house. This floor also featured additional rooms of various description, including a walk-through pantry that I occasionally used as a short cut to get from the music room to my great-grandmother's kitchen.

Nanny's kitchen was an anachronistic holdover from an earlier time period. At one side of the room sat a large metal washer with a hand-crank wringer into which clothing was fed until the last of the water had been strangled out of them. I always watched in fascination as my grandmother cranked the handle, but was continually warned not to get my fingers too close to the wringers for fear they might get swallowed up— yet another device waiting to attack little boys. In the back hall just off the kitchen sat an old wooden ice box. The ice man came every few days to deliver more ice, as Nanny slid the tray out from under the heavy wooden cabinet to empty water from the melting ice. Even after a gas-powered refrigerator was installed in the kitchen, this new "modern" device was still referred to by Nanny as the "ice box."

From the first-floor kitchen, a large sun room led out to the backyard which, for the first few years of my life, was my playground. In the middle of the backyard stood a peach tree with plenty of fruit, free for the picking. If only I had been tall enough to reach it. (And if only I had liked peaches.) At the far end of the yard was a tall, rocky cliff made of puddingstone, a natural three-mile-thick conglomerate layer consisting largely of diamictite mixed with quartzite and granite, and a unique geological feature for which Roxbury is known. Some scientific literature, in fact, refers to the unique substance as "Roxbury Puddingstone." To a four-year-old, this outcropping rose to an enormous height, although to an adult, it no doubt appeared somewhat less dramatic. Beyond the top of this rock formation sat the home of our neighbor, Mrs. Capucci, although despite its being perched at a somewhat higher elevation, it was Nanny's gigantic home that dominated the entire neighborhood.

Being the center of the neighborhood, however, had its disadvantages. At the front corner of our large yard an enormous tree was partially encircled by a waist-high concrete wall at the intersection of the two streets. Not only was this a central landmark, but it provided a perfect spot for neighborhood hoodlums to gather and smoke cigarettes. This was my great-aunt Nonny's signal to emerge from the house and chase them from their perch.

Other characters who frequented the neighborhood became scary, exaggerated freaks when fed by the nightmarish distortions of my four-year-old mind. These aberrations, no doubt, were the result of the nearly constant awareness that I was never far from the fiery monster dwelling in the dungeon. One such individual that caused me uneasiness was what my cousin had told me was a two-headed lady. The middle-aged black woman, (referred to in those days as Negro or sometimes worse) occasionally passed by the house balancing what appeared to be a second head. Looking back at this from these many decades later, I realize that the additional cranium she kept wrapped in a kerchief above her primary head was probably a gigantic accumulation of her own hair that had grown until it had reached the size of a huge beehive.

Another all too familiar sight was that of the hunchback man dressed always in black who shuffled slowly past our house on a regular basis. He never spoke but looked straight ahead as if he were in a trance. Even some of my adult relatives stopped whatever they were doing to suspiciously watch him pass.

It has now been well over half a century since the sound of my tiny bare feet have been heard running down the halls and into relatives' kitchens. I find myself now, however, in the unlikely position of sitting on the front steps of that same grand old house. I'm on the very steps that saw ancestors come and go, that felt the veil of my mother's wedding dress brush past, and where, after a day of hard work, countless relatives relaxed to watch the neighborhood activity on Cedar and Highland Streets. The big tree on the corner is gone, but the house appears almost exactly as it does in the old sepia photograph I hold in my hand. The big granite posts still mark the entrance to the front yard. The railings and porch trim look identical. And the same windows mark the rooms that bore witness to births, deaths, weddings, and Christmases past.

Sitting beside me is the current owner and resident of the old house, Mrs. Jones. When I walked up to the front door without warning and rang the doorbell, she tentatively cracked open the door, and slowly peered out. She then began what sounded like a prepared and rehearsed speech.

"No, I don't want to sell the house."

After introducing myself and assuring her that I was not in the market for real estate, I held up my old family photo album and pointed to a picture of the house taken in the 1940s.

"I used to live here a long time ago," I continued. "This was my great-grandmother's house and I lived here along with countless relatives."

Intrigued, Mrs. Jones emerged and sat down on the steps, inviting me to do the same. I relayed some of the memories I had of events in the house, neighborhood characters, climbing the puddingstone cliff out back, and looking out the attic window onto the fire escape. She, in turn, told me about some of the renovations she and her husband had been planning, while keeping the original look of the building intact. We looked through the album one page at a time pointing out features of the old house, both inside and out that were still exactly the same, or that had been modified only slightly in some way.

The basic configuration of rooms has remained the same, the ornate woodwork and trim has been preserved, and the yard, aside from missing the big tree, had not appreciably changed from what I could tell. I told her about the hoodlums who used to loiter by the concrete wall on the corner and smoke. I told her about family picnics out back under the peach tree. I pointed out the building across the street that had been my great-grandfather's grocery store starting back in the 1920s. I informed her that my grandfather had made the parquet floors in the big parlor where my mother had been married as well as many of the other rooms.

I told her about my mother's memories of the horse-drawn wagon that plodded up Cedar Street delivering milk. She recalls that the milkman would approach the house with his delivery while the horse, knowing the route, would continue on its own, stopping at the next delivery site. My mother also remembers walking to nearby Fenway Park to attend Boston Red Sox games where her admission fee was ten cents.

As we turned the brittle pages of the album, one old photo after another sparked memories which I immediately shared. I reminisced about family celebrations and parties around the holidays, and told her about some of my relatives and ancestors who called this place home. I told her about the men of the family playing horseshoes out back while the ladies sat on the front porch exactly where we now found ourselves sitting.

I didn't, however, tell her about the monster in the dungeon. I'll let her find that out for herself.

Family members under the peach tree pose for a photo taken from the puddingstone cliff., ca. 1950

The author sits atop the famed puddingstone cliff, ca. 1950

It's About Time

My fifth birthday was a milestone I thought would never arrive. For weeks, my parents had been prepping me for this special occasion and reminding me that shortly, when someone asked my age, I would be able to answer by holding up all the fingers of one hand.

"Pretty soon you're going to be five," they'd gush. "Then, just one more year after that and you'll be ready for school. You're getting to be a big boy."

They made it sound so epic that I could not begin to imagine myself at such an extreme age. But blowing out the meager collection of candles on my birthday cake, I was already thinking ahead. I imagined what it would possibly be like in one more year to reach the ripe old age of six and be heading off to attend school. I had previously met a couple of six-year-olds who embodied what I considered to be a noticeable difference in development. Their level of sophistication was markedly beyond my young age. Not only were they taller with bigger bicycles, but they were allowed to cross the street by themselves.

An entire year, however, was a span of time I found

difficult to fathom. The overwhelming duration of a year was perceived as monumental. This bewildering comprehension of time is not surprising given that the duration of the single year necessary to get from age five to age six represented, at that point in time, fully twenty percent of my entire existence. This enormous span of evolvement had occurred only a few times in my young life. Quite different, I would later discover, than the minuscule percentage of my lifetime represented by a year at say, age sixty. But, for now, a whole year would remain an enormous portion of my current lifetime.

It is not surprising then, that it took me forever to get through the first grade. I remember sitting obediently in Mrs. McClain's classroom wondering how grownups ever got to the point of bossing us little kids around, while doing whatever they wanted whenever they wanted to do it. It seemed a fantasy that they themselves had ever been children. Trying to visualize my parents playing with blocks and riding tricycles proved futile. No more could I imagine my dad playing with toy cowboy pistols than I could picture myself jumping off a building and flying through the air like Superman. The vast amount of time it would take to get from where I now sat to sitting in the driver's seat of a car seemed a stretch of time approaching forever. Even the amount of time it would take to get to the second grade seemed inconceivable.

Secretly watching third and fourth-graders on the school bus was a clandestine activity I often undertook. They did not seem so out of reach from my current standing, but even that relatively short time frame I found difficult to imagine. It was much easier to imagine them, not so long ago, being in the first grade, still learning how to write the alphabet, than it was for me to project myself into that far-distant third-grade future.

As I became a little older, it somehow became easier to relate to the passage of time. The span of a year was compressed into an easily perceivable duration. And as more time passed, the years seemed to get progressively shorter in duration. It almost seemed as if I made it from eighth grade all the way through high school graduation in only two years—something my report card would indicate was definitely not possible.

When I entered college, the duration of a year continued to shrink, and this distortion of time was becoming more noticeable. By that time, the passage of a year represented a mere five percent of my life span—a much smaller percentage than had been the case as a child. This caused me to view each year as a shorter length of time. My four college years were so much fun, in fact, that I wished the opposite had been the case. But time marched on.

With college graduation behind me, time seemed to be speeding up at an accelerated rate. Anticipation was much diminished when compared with the endless time I spent as a kid, for example, waiting for Christmas to arrive each year. Its arrival had always seemed so far off and the wait interminable. Back then, the days seemed to go on and on without end making it seem that Christmas would never get here. I don't mean to say that as I got older, events were not anticipated. They were, and at times, with great enthusiasm. It's just that the time spent looking forward to an event seemed to be cut short and pass by more quickly. Now, as I began my career, events and milestones in my life seemed to approach with little warning.

I'd wake up one morning and think to myself, *"Oh my God! Christmas is next week already."*

That process of acceleration has not slowed. Time continues to become more distorted with each year that passes, and I sometimes marvel at the pronounced phenomenon. The more years that pass, the more I begin to use decades as a measure rather than just years. My mental time frame has become extended as years have become condensed. Events that occurred a decade or more ago suddenly don't seem that far distant. Watching time from this vantage point has led to expressions such as *"Where did the time go?"* It's something that becomes noticeable only as years advance. That's why you'll never hear a young kid utter the words "Time flies!"

Even history itself begins to take on a compressed time frame when viewed from the vantage point of one's own advancing age. When I was in school, the Civil War seemed like ancient history. I'd have to go back in time nearly ten of my own lifetimes to approach that period in history. Despite the fact that time is absolute, it appears more and more relative. The time that has passed since the Civil War I now am able to measure as the extent of merely a couple of my lifetimes. The Civil War seems more recent to me than it did when I was a child, even though I'm now so many more decades removed from that event than I was then. Time is definitely shrinking.

It makes me wonder what world-changing events will occur soon after the brief span of my lifetime here on earth has come to a glorious conclusion. Will there be cures for every dreaded disease known to man? Will we discover alien life on another planet? Will drivers have finally figured out how to use turn signals? Looking back at other lives in history, if certain individuals could have survived just a few more years, they would have been in disbelief at what was to occur.

Consider the fact that man walked on the moon a mere sixty-six years after the Wright brothers' first flight. To a six-year-old, that seems like a very long time—more than ten lifetimes, to be exact. Chances are, to you reading this account, however, this stretch of time is seen in quite the opposite way. In my case, less than one lifetime. George Washington, too, would be amazed were he able to look back at what occurred only a few short years after he was gone. Our first president, for example, had no idea that dinosaurs ever existed, as the first fossils were not identified until 1830, a mere three decades after his passing.

So now, with yet another birthday only a few months away, I'm faced with a dilemma. Should I sign up for the three-year telephone plan, or go for a one-year commitment?

The To-Do List

My familiar handwritten list of ongoing tasks and chores is always with me. It accompanies me when I go visit friends. It's with me when I walk downtown for coffee, and it's with me when I go out to dinner. My to-do list is a constant companion. Even if I'm someplace where I'm unable to accomplish tasks on my list, it's with me just in case I think of something to be added to the list. Reminders are everywhere, and I wouldn't want to miss an opportunity to make my list even longer than it already is. How was I to know, for example, when the waiter at the restaurant brought me the bill that it would remind me that I needed to call my friend Bill. Or that when that bird left a deposit on my car windshield that it would remind me I needed to make a bank deposit.

Most entries remain on my to-do list for only a day or two before being purged with the stroke of a pen. Crossing items off my to-do list is a common and satisfying occurrence, although a few of the items have been simply recopied from my previous list as the small piece of paper inevitably fills up before I've had a chance to complete all the tasks on the list. A few constantly recurring items are perpetually copied from list to list to list as they remain uncompleted for one reason or another. "Paint kitchen" for example, might hold the record for appearing on the most to-do lists. If "paint kitchen" were a song, it would have been on the hit parade chart for months. Projects like this, however, recur on the list because, unlike daily chores, they are usually very large, long-term projects.

Each item on my list is kept as brief as possible so as not to fill the paper too quickly. Lengthy wording and explanations serve only to take up unnecessary space, prompting the need for a new list. So in an effort to keep each entry to a single line, I use shorthand descriptions—yard work, haircut, car stuff, and so on. Generally, one or two words is enough to remind me what needs to be done without a wordy explanation. I know that "car stuff" for example, means I need to have the tires rotated, the oil changed, and then run it through the car wash. Yard work means cut the grass and rake leaves.

But occasionally, an item on my to-do list remains for such a long time that I actually forget what my shorthand label means. An entry that reads "photos" has continued to baffle me. Are there photos of something that I'm supposed to take? Did I intend to post some photos on Facebook? And an entry that reads simply "birthday card" also continues to confuse me. Who was I supposed to buy a birthday card for? Did I forget someone's birthday? If that's the case, I'm sure the day has passed and I should remove the item, but it remains on my list in hopes that I'll at least remember whose special day I ignored.

Likewise, I have no idea why the entry "Write To-Do List" should appear on my to-do list, but I repeatedly copy it to each subsequent list hoping I'll remember why I thought it necessary to include the self-fulfilling entry in the first place. There must have been a good reason at the time, but each time I recopy it the logic escapes me. Perhaps it was simply so I could have the immediate satisfaction of scribbling it out as soon as I make my new list. There's a very satisfying feeling of accomplishment that comes with the purging of each completed task, so for the time being, I'll continue to include it and then immediately cross it off.

For a while, I tried keeping a digital to-do list on my phone, but deleting a completed task is not nearly as satisfying as taking a pen and scribbling out the entry with emphatic black strokes. It's for this reason that I also don't simply put a polite little check mark next to completed tasks. A paper list full of assertive and conspicuous scribbles is much more gratifying and reminds me that I've actually done something. Once a task is done, I want to see a reminder of my success. The heavy strokes that obliterate these completed tasks are just that. They symbolize successful completion more than merely deleting something on my phone ever could. Once deleted on a digital device, there's no visual reminder that I've been successful at finishing a task.

This, however, is a double-edged sword. If I attempt to complete a task, only to fail, I'm faced with a constant reminder on each subsequent list until satisfactory results are achieved. If I do a poor job of painting the kitchen, (not that that would ever happen) I'm constantly reminded of my failure by the entry that reads "paint kitchen AGAIN."

Some listings change as progress is made on long-term projects. When I was replacing a section of fencing in the backyard, for example, the specific task on my list reflected the stage at which the project currently stood. "Measure fence" became "buy wood." "Buy wood" became "cut fencing." "Cut fencing" then became "paint fence slats," which in turn was changed to "install fence," and so on. The reason for these ongoing modifications is so that a project doesn't seem as daunting. If the task were simply labeled "replace fencing," it might continually be overlooked as too big a project to tackle on any specific day. It might just be copied to my next list, and then to the one after that. When large projects are broken down into bite-size pieces, they are seen as more manageable and consequently get done faster.

When I was in the business world this is also how things were done. Jobs were not simply listed by their over-arching titles and left to plod along in hopes of timely completion. They were broken down into stages of their development process and weekly status reports were due each Monday. The reports not only listed each particular job, but also detailed the stage at which the projects currently stood and the needs going forward. A checklist of items under each job provided not only easy assessment of a project's progress, but detailed specific tasks and responsibilities while moving toward completion.

In the columns next to each job, various milestones were listed along with deadlines for each task. A typical job might show a series of ongoing tasks such as input needed, initial design, responsibility, client presentation, revisions, and so on. In the columns next to each job were listed the steps needed for completion and the individual responsible for those particular steps. These official reports might just as easily have been called "The Weekly To-Do List." Business being what it is, however, the overly-serious documents featured the self-important heading "Project Status Report." The document I now carry around in my pocket is a little less formal. And I'm always the individual responsible for the tasks.

As I sit here, I remove the list from my pocket just to see if there's something I should be doing instead of writing yet another stupid story. I scan the handwritten list of items— order vitamins, dry cleaning, vacuum car, pay cable bill, iron shirts, call Mom. Clear and unambiguous directives. For the umpteenth time however, my eyes fall upon the recurring item "write to-do list," and then it hits me. I finally remember what it means! It's not a self-fulfilling item whose inclusion is obsolete the instant it's written. I realize it's a reminder that I should write a short story about my to-do list. I also realize that I've just done it. As I write this final sentence, I take out my pen and scribble a dark and emphatic line through the perplexing listing. And as I cross out this perpetually confusing entry, I hear myself announce out loud the words that herald its successful completion.

"To Do. Ta-Da!"

Subtle Butter

Mr. Butler stood before the class at a total loss for words. He shifted his weight from one foot to the other and repeatedly cleared his throat.

"Ahem. Uhhh... Very interesting. What did you say it was called again?"

I had just finished performing an original poem to my college English class. I say "performing" because I was presenting the results of our class assignment in partnership with three other students. And I use the word "poem" though there were no long rhyming stanzas with flowery language or sentiments. Each "verse," if you will, was no longer than a few syllables. In so doing, we had invented a completely new form of the literary medium.

This unique form of poetry required two people to read at the same time. However, the words each presenter spoke were slightly different, thus creating a certain audio resonance—at times harmonic, and at times, very discordant.

For example, one reader might read the word "subtle." The other might, at exactly the same instant, read the word "butter." When overlapped at precisely the same time, the two words, "subtle" and "butter" create a dissonance that is slightly jarring to the ear. The resulting sound of the overlapping syllables clash in a vibration akin to a musical instrument that is slightly out of tune. Other words read in tandem might blend beautifully, having the opposite effect, and resulting in a more harmonic and pleasing sound. Think of it like rhyming, only concurrent. Unfortunately, because of their unique configuration, the specific poems cannot be presented here in writing without completely losing their desired effect. It is an oral medium only.

Our decidedly hyper-analysis of the *Subtle Butter* poem's structure reveals an alignment of the sound "ut," heard in each word, while the other dissonant overlapping syllables clash. The result is an ambiguous perception of which word you are actually hearing. As we explained to the class, it is also important for the listener to be aware of the feeling each combination of words generates within his vibrational field. We provided this in-depth, technical analysis to Mr. Butler to demonstrate our diligence in analyzing the underlying structure of this unique form of alliteration.

The name we had coined for this original style of composition was *"Simultaneous Poetry."* Timing was critical for this new art-form to work, and required rehearsals on our part prior to demonstrating our genius in front of the class.

In an art college where creativity is encouraged at all levels, breaking the rules was typically rewarded. Mr. Butler, however, still at a loss for words and still unsure whether we were indeed demonstrating our genius or simply making fun of his serious assignment, grudgingly gave us a "B" for our efforts.

We never had any delusions about our new form of poetry catching on and becoming commonplace among the literary icons of the nineteen-sixties. Having presented a few more simultaneous poems, we took our seats that day amid a few snickers and the perplexed expressions of our classmates. It was an experiment that was destined to be remembered for, perhaps, only a few days. Some fifty years later, however, whenever I get together with my fellow presenters, we still laugh about our inroads into a literary breakthrough that is still waiting to break through.

The Urge to Purge

Once in a while I feel the urge to throw stuff out to make room for more stuff. Some of it goes right into the trash, while some is donated to Goodwill or The Salvation Army. Why shouldn't someone else have the pleasure of squeezing into my pleated dress pants that went out of style in 1985? And old VHS tapes. There must be some use for these things.

As I go through my bedroom closets, old chests, and crusty boxes in the basement I come across things I didn't even know I had or where I got them. My rule of thumb is: *If I haven't used an item for at least two decades, I'll consider getting rid of it in a few more years.* There are some things that may once again be of some use if I hold on to them long enough. My old 8-track cartridges, for example, last saw service in 1981, but you never know.

Now in no way would I be considered a hoarder. I don't have narrow pathways between floor to ceiling stacks of old magazines or that I can't bear to throw away used pizza boxes thinking they might one day come in handy to hold, I don't know... old record albums? I am not a hoarder. I have, however, always been a collector. Some of my collections might seem a bit odd to people who pursue the more traditional activities of collecting stamps or coins. To them I say, "How predictable."

Now I have nothing against those particular hobbies, but it just seems very ordinary. To me, an assemblage of more unusual items just seems more interesting. Any single item of unusual character may be of some interest as an oddity worthy of, perhaps, a second look. But even rather mundane items when gathered together in an entire collection of similar pieces, take on a whole new life and become worthy, in some cases, of a museum, or at least an interesting display.

On one of my bookshelves at home is a large book in which are pictured hundreds of collections of the most ordinary items that, by themselves, no one would consider even of passing interest. However, the way in which these items have been grouped with similar items causes the entire assemblage to be viewed in a whole new context. A framed assortment of wooden rulers with advertising becomes an artistic panel. A jar of vintage glass marbles becomes worthy of a place on the mantle. Dozens of imprinted wine corks create a beautiful mosaic when framed together. One collection pictured in the book is of vintage plastic whistles which takes on a whimsical look. There's even a page that shows a collection of bride and groom wedding cake figures that, by themselves would be unremarkable, but as a collection, is fascinating.

Some of my collections began decades ago and are added to whenever the opportunity presents itself. My huge collection of antique pinback buttons began in the 1960s with interesting flea market finds. Most of the individual specimens in this particular collection are now over one hundred years

old. But it's their colorful graphics and images that attract me. For this reason, I shy away from political buttons which tend to feature only bland lettering on flat colored backgrounds. A "We Like Ike" button from the 1950s may be of some passing interest from a historical perspective, but there is no graphic or artistic intrigue to such a piece. A multi-color button from the early 1900s, however, that reads "Honorary Pilot Tydol Flying Airship" and features an image of a huge blimp with the "Flying A" gasoline logo emblazoned on its side is a beautiful piece of art and much more interesting. (Sorry Ike.) The full-color images on many of my buttons are beautifully detailed, and look as though they just came out of a time machine.

Of similar interest are my sets of colorful buttons from the American Pepsin Gum Company that, in the 1920s, came one in every pack of their chewing gum, and featured a different cartoon character of the day. Again, these have much more allure than plain words spelling out the name of some political candidate. The full-color artwork and renderings on many of these pieces dating as far back as the late 1800s have not only a historic interest, but are charming in their detail and character.

Having spent my entire career in the field of advertising, I am drawn to the pinback buttons that advertise early products or services. Many of the buttons in my vast collection feature products that have not been available for many decades. It is this look back in the history of product advertising that I find so compelling. Product images and sayings of extinct companies such as Little Jockey Cigarettes, Snaider's Syrup, Samson Wind Mills, Ceresota Flour, and the ever-popular DeLaval Cream Separator hearken back to a bygone era as reminders of a different world.

Other collections in my possession are also examples of early advertising. My collection of vintage fly swatters with advertising are reminders of the varied media by which early companies advertised their products. For Peletier's Hardware Store, I can understand their decision to put their name on this particular advertising medium. But why Gerber's Baby Food would want to associate their product with the squashing of helpless flies leaves me at a loss.

I also collect vintage postcards with several sub-category themes. There's my postcard collection of ugly 1950s roadside motels known as motor courts, and another one featuring diners. There's even a set of postcards featuring giant boulders with names. Apparently, before television, a favorite pass-time was to discover huge rocks whose forms resembled some object and then name the rocks accordingly. Thus, *The Devil's Anvil, Elephant Rock,* and *Cathedral Rock.* Precariously perched boulders the size of houses in several states also share the name *Balance Rock.*

One huge box I come across every now and then in my basement is something I call my "twenty-year box." For decades I've used it as a repository for small items that I think will eventually become curiosities. Nothing in the box will probably ever be worth anything. That's not the point. The pieces I throw into the box are items that might at least be of some passing interest twenty years or so after they're stashed away in the box. As companies come and go, and as things change over the years, I might salvage some small item as a reminder of the past and throw it into the twenty-year box.

For example, when Johnson's Baby Powder retired their tin containers in favor of plastic, I grabbed one of the soon-to-be obsolete metal ones to save. When Esso Gasoline changed its name to Exxon, I added my expired Esso credit card to the box. Likewise, the box became a home for my old MasterCharge card when they adopted the new name of Master*Card*.

There are small, plastic premiums that came free in packages of Salada Tea in the 1980s, and give-aways from other companies that are no longer around. Companies like Life Magazine and Twist Lemon-flavored Cigarettes. These things I've decided to retain. They don't take up much room in the basement, and my kids might one day enjoy looking at them one by one as they hurl them into the dumpster.

I've occasionally purged some of these things at yard sales and sold some of the better items to antique dealers. For the most part though, my collections consist of small pieces, unlike some people I've met who have made the questionable decision to take up valuable space with large collections of bulky things like old typewriters, pinball machines and guitars.

A few years ago a wealthy doctor in a neighboring town had an enormous auction to purge some of his collections. Two huge barns were filled with antique toys, architectural salvage, stained glass windows, marble statuary, and antique furniture. Several acres of fields around his mansion were strewn with collections of antique automobiles, wooden boats, stacks of automobile wheel rims, more than a hundred bicycles, and even a collection of outboard motors. Anyone who considers himself a hoarder would only have had to attend his auction to realize that the good doctor had totally upstaged you.

Just a few of over a hundred bikes up for auction at the doctor's estate.

The first day of the auction was for previewing only as curious people wandered the expansive grounds of his estate. Given this entire day to look around, however, it would still have been impossible to view every piece on the auction block. Auctions America, the Indiana-based company enlisted to run the event, employed over twenty individuals who, attired in their matching blue shirts, passed out listing sheets and answered questions of potential buyers who would make their hopeful bids on the following day.

The second day saw thousands of items auctioned off as several auctioneers worked simultaneously in different sec-

Rows of countless automobile wheel rims up for auction.

tions of the property, each offering separate categories of items for bidding. Many buyers showed up from out of state with flatbed trailers on which to haul away large purchases. A huge circus-size food tent provided meals and snacks to hungry bidders, as the proceedings would last until well into the evening of the second day.

Seeing the extent to which the doctor had amassed his vast and extravagant hoards made me realize how much of a novice I was with my meager collections of small curiosities. I realized I had a long way to go before anyone could accurately have characterized me as a hoarder. I am not a hoarder. Nevertheless, just so there's no confusion, I'm letting you know that I'm thinking about getting rid of my Polaroid camera. I'm just waiting to see if this whole digital camera fad catches on.

Civilization

When Gandhi was asked what he thought of western civilization he is reported to have said, "I think it would be a good idea."

In this country we tend to think of ourselves as the pinnacle of technological advancement. We imagine that people the world over look to us with envy and wonder how we became so highly evolved. It is more likely that they marvel at how little time it took us to become so uppity and conceited having all our priorities backwards. This experiment we call democracy has been in existence only a little more than two hundred years. And it has seen problems and changes. Sure, we've developed an economy that surpasses all the other countries on the planet. We're responsible for much of the technology the world now runs on. We've invented or discovered the majority of advancements seen in the last century. And we take credit for most of what generally passes as progress.

Our status as a highly evolved society may seem true when viewed through the eyes of those who judge by the power of our military or the size of our bank accounts. But

Gandhi would look at this "progress" and believe we're going in the wrong direction. People starving or deprived of medical treatment and proper housing are not signs of an advanced civilization any more than slurring your words and falling down a staircase would be a sign of sobriety. He would remind us that a society should be judged by the quality of life of its poorest citizens. If anyone is to be left out, society as a whole will suffer.

What have we done as a nation to spread our good fortune to others around the globe, ensuring that everyone has access to food, education, technology, healthcare and other things most of us take for granted? I'm not saying we've done nothing to help the citizens of third-world countries. There are charities and even government programs that issue everything from disaster relief to food and medicine. Yet there are still those, even in our own country, who are deprived of those aspects of what we consider to be basic.

We may be guilty of uncivilized behavior on an individual basis as well. We tend to think of ourselves as better, smarter, and more successful than our neighbors because we may have a newer car, a bigger house, or designer sunglasses. This is what Gandhi viewed as some of the many horrors of modern civilization. All of this, he believed, comes at the expense of ethical and spiritual values, which he also believed, are more important.

Our individual success should not come at the expense of true happiness. Technological advancement should not be at the expense of personal interaction and connection. I have seen too many people working to the point of isolation from others to make a buck. I have seen them focus on nothing but money. That's not the hallmark of civilization.

Now, I'm not saying that we should all live in tents and wear ragged clothing, although, when I traveled through India I saw much of this. Those people, however, seemed genuinely happy and I watched them interact as they helped each other load horse-drawn wagons with vegetables and firewood. I saw them communicating face to face, not texting on phones. They cooked over open fires and seemed to be sharing food with others walking by on the dirt streets. They were not using what they had to separate themselves from others less fortunate. They were using what they had to bond with others and share. This is what Gandhi would call civilization—people interacting in a meaningful way for the benefit of all, helping, sharing, and spreading happiness.

I also do not mean to say that everyone must live in a mansion and own three luxury automobiles. Nor, however, do I mean that *no one* should be able to do so. Individuals should be able to reap the rewards of success and enjoy the material things they work hard to manifest. The promise of individual success is something that often contributes to the advancement of all. Inventions and discoveries that make everyone's life a little better, safer, and happier have largely been made possible by those throughout history who have often been personally compensated beyond all measure. To them I offer, a well-deserved "thank you." Those who have devoted entire lives to cures for disease, advancement in mass communications, safer methods of construction and travel, more efficient methods of food production and distribution, as well as life-changing advances like electricity and refrigeration have deserved to be well-paid for their contributions to society.

But don't mistake a civilized culture for the amount of wealth or hi-tech inventions at one's disposal. The true measure of civilization is much simpler than that. It's not measured by what you have, but rather by how you act. One's behavior toward others is a much more accurate indicator of civilization. It can be found at the root of simple, everyday actions like holding the door open for a stranger at the store. It can be shown by not cutting someone off in traffic. And when someone cuts *you* off in traffic, the civilized response would be to not give them the finger.

This may seem to fly in the face of Sigmund Freud's declaration that "the first human who hurled an insult instead of a stone was the founder of civilization." Freud may have believed that giving someone the finger was a perfectly acceptable insult in civilized society, and I suppose it is better than throwing a rock at someone. But I would go one better and say let's not give people the finger, let's give them a hand. It's in our power to contribute to civilization by doing just that whenever possible.

But it's not just how one individual acts toward another individual that determines the degree of civilization. We as individuals also have a role to play in how society as a whole either encourages or limits the advancement of civilization. When we as individuals turn our heads and refuse to see pollution, waste, and selfishness by countries, companies or industries, we are contributing to an "uncivilized" society. When we turn our backs on those who are victims of discrimination we are suppressing the rise of civilization and have ourselves to blame. Our role may seem small in the scheme of things, but we all have a part to play in stopping waste and climate change, and helping to bring about cleaner air, cleaner water, and the equal inclusion of all members of society. Each of these factors has a bearing on the well-being of all. "A rising tide lifts all boats" seems an appropriate metaphor for a civilization in which no one is left out.

Maybe Gandhi was right about western civilization. Perhaps it would be a good idea.

The End

It is reported that when Bob Hope's wife asked him where he wanted to be buried, he replied, "Surprise me."

The famous Irish poet, Oscar Wilde, lying on his death-bed in 1900, is reported to have said, "Either this wallpaper goes or I do."

And the dying words of Mexican Revolutionary General Pancho Villa were "Don't let it end like this. Tell them I said something."

Our morbid fascination with leaving something that will live on after we no longer do, is a curious, if not meaning-less undertaking (pun intended). We like to believe that our brief lives will hold meaning for the generations who come after us. But the undeniable truth is that it will not take long for the memory of who we were to become a forgotten relic.

Generations pass quickly. What we think of as a long life, in the scheme of things, is no more than a blip on the radar of time. A mere few generations after we draw our last breath, the life deemed so important as it was being lived will be rel-egated to a meaningless footnote. Unless we happen to be a president, a king, or a famous rock'n roll singer, those whose lives begin after our lives end will not care about anything we did. To the generations born after our demise, we will be just a name. And even that is optimistic. Ask anyone the name of their great-great grandfather, and you will no doubt be met with a blank stare.

I am made aware of this as I walk past cemeteries filled with row upon row of neglected headstones leaning and sinking into the ground. Many of the names carved into the stone a century or two ago are worn so smooth that the lettering now resembles indistinct ancient fossils. The cold, gray slate marking the spot under which lies some forgotten soul, is a reminder of how quickly even we ourselves will become anonymous.

The former individual lying just below the name and dates carved into the decaying stone no doubt believed this would be the spot where generations of his descendants would gather to remember him—that the stone, like a bookmark, would forever mark his place in history. Now it is merely an obstacle the grounds crew must negotiate and avoid with their lawnmowers.

Over the years I have been able to discover the headstones of some of my distant ancestors. I am quite certain, however, that I am in the extreme minority of individuals inclined to do so. I see no others winding their way among rows of tilted markers. The carved names of my long-dead ancestors, however, are nothing more than a curiosity to me. A faceless entry on a genealogy chart.

Yet the trend to leave one's mark continues to this day. The pressing need to shout from the grave, "I was here," bears witness to the self-importance of those who now lie in eternal obscurity.

One has only to look to the pyramids of Egypt to realize that this is not a modern phenomenon. Since the beginning of history, man has devised countless physical objects created in the hope that the deceased individual will be perpetually remembered by continuing to take up space on our crowded planet.

Even much of the residue resulting from cremations is placed in urns or in cemetery vaults as a physical reminder. Those that sit atop a mantle or bookshelf next to cousin Billy's Little League trophy will likely remain there indefinitely. No descendant is willing to be the one who finally decides to throw Grampa Edward into the garbage along with last night's leftover casserole.

Now, however, a new chapter in the history of entombment is beginning to be written. The state of Washington has become first in the nation to make human composting legal. The Seattle-based company, Recompose, is now turning human bodies into compost by means of a process that is actually good for the environment. Even cremation, because of the burning involved, cannot lay claim to this distinction. But now, as he is mixed with wood chips, straw, and alfalfa, Grampa Edward can actually help to fertilize new growth, making the planet a healthier place for those of us who continue to live. As of this writing, however, this environmentally-conscious alternative remains available in one state only.

As far as the final disposition of my own remains is concerned, given that a pyramid is financially unfeasible, and until the day when human bodies are disposed of by simply shooting them into space, I have decided to be cremated. What becomes of the approximately half gallon of remaining ash matters little to me. I will leave that up to those lucky ones who survive me. I have made it clear that what becomes of the residue that was once me is totally their decision.

As long as I don't hear any flushing sounds.

Order other books by this author at www.AuthorDavidRandom.com

DEFYING GRAVITY

A collection of humorous true stories from the author's long career at Boston and New York-based ad agencies.

GULLIBLE'S TRAVELS

A collection of humorous short stories based on the author's impressionable youth.

CONNECTED

In this fictional crime novel an eyewitness to a murder comes forward and the killer confesses. But there's a problem. The eyewitness and the murderer are conjoined twins. An unprecedented legal dilemma ensues as the killer cannot be imprisoned without also locking up his innocent conjoined twin. Can there possibly be any satisfactory resolution?

Connected was awarded the coveted Pinnacle Book Achievement Award for crime fiction.

CPSIA information can be obtained
at www.ICGtesting.com
Printed in the USA
BVHW080955191221
624255BV00001B/36